TROUBLE IN HADES

QUEENS OF OLYMPUS

ARIZONA TAPE

Copyright © 2022 by Arizona Tape

All rights reserved. No part of this publication or cover may be reproduced, distributed, or transmitted in any form or by any means, including photocopying, recording, or other electronic or mechanical methods, without the prior written permission of the publisher, except in the case of brief quotations embodied in critical reviews and certain other noncommercial uses permitted by copyright law.

Trouble In Hades is a work of fiction. Names, characters, businesses, places, events, locales, and incidents are either the products of the author's imagination or used in a fictitious manner. Any resemblance to actual persons, living or dead, or actual events is purely coincidental. Individuals depicted in the images are models and used solely for illustrative purposes.

For permission requests or other inquiries, write to Arizona Tape at arizonatape@arizonatape.com .

Cover by Vampari Designs

https://arizonatape.com/vamparidesigns

BLURB

Ruling the Underworld is a job no one wants...until now.

As the new Hades, Maia is determined to make a difference, even if the current Persephone doesn't believe her.

There's nothing that Penelope hates more than a new Hades, especially when they make her job as the Persephone harder.

But something about this time is different. Maybe it's finally time for the problems in the Underworld to be fixed...

-

Trouble In Hades is a fantasy twist on the classic Greek myth of Hades and Persephone with an f/f romantic subplot. It's the first book in the Queens of Olympus series following various heroines in classic Greek God and Goddess retellings.

ONE

Maia

There wasn't a child on Olympus who grew up without hearing stories about the Underworld. Still, nothing could have prepared me for my own descent. The black horses in front of the large carriage trampled impatiently, urging me to get in as they vibrated the ground around me.

With a last look at the Overworld, I climbed on board. I sat down on the velvet bench and the carriage bolted forward, encouraged by the relentless whips of the driver. I pushed one of the little curtains to the side just in time to see the ground open up and swallow us. Darkness engulfed me for the longest time and a chill wrapped around me like a gentle hug.

A hard thud shook the carriage and I almost fell off my seat. The rhythm of the wheels underneath changed and I knew we were back on solid ground. Intrigued, I returned to the window for my first view of the Underworld.

Green smoke dissipated as the horses raced through it, leaving a clear view of the world around me. Large fields and orchards stretched over rolling hills as far as I could see. A large river cut the landscape in two and massive ships slowly charted their course through the murky water.

My first view of the Styx.

The carriage thundered along the river of the dead and a black castle appeared on the horizon. In the blink of an eye, the distance disappeared and I was flying through an ostentatious iron gate. Separated from the rest of the Underworld, we crossed large private gardens to the entrance of the palace.

We came to a halt and my stomach finally stopped turning. Thoroughly shaken, I can't help but wonder if my organs are still in the right place.

The side door opened and my driver pulled down the little steps for me. She gave me a wry smile and a deep bow. "After you, Your Darkness."

I winced at the strange title but I wasn't sure what I could do about it. I stayed silent as I got out of the carriage, relieved to have solid ground under my feet. Hopefully, I wouldn't have to do that every day.

The driver bowed again before jumping back on the carriage and whipping the four black horses into motion. The beasts thundered away, leaving me in front of the largest palace I'd ever seen. Expertly built out of black iron and steel, the whole building towered over me with intricate gold detailing and all kinds of terrifying statues. Not exactly cosy.

I gulped as the large front door swung open by itself. I shouldn't fear it, or anything really. After all, I was Hades, master of the dead. Ruler of the Underworld and everyone in it. Still... It would take some time to get used to that.

With a last look at the gardens behind me, I entered the palace. The front doors slammed shut behind me and the sound echoed into the wide halls. My new home...

I looked around, unsure what to do. There was nobody here to greet me or help me out. Not the warm welcome I'd hoped for.

Just as I found the confidence to venture into the castle, a figure appeared out of nowhere. At first glance, it looked to be a young, beautiful woman clad in nothing more than a couple of well placed white rags.

The nymph swayed towards me with a wide smile and fell down at my feet. "Welcome to your home. I'm Erebus, your humble servant and caretaker of the palace. What can I do to please you, Your Darkness?"

"Your Darkness?" I repeated, not enamoured with it.

The nymph smiled. "I can call you whatever you like."

"Well, my name is Maia. How about that?"

"As you wish. Maia," she tried out, my name rolling off her tongue with a seductive hiss. "I live to serve and please you." A rather awkward statement given how little clothing she was wearing. She noticed me staring and giggled coyly. "Do you approve of my appearance?"

I hesitated.

The woman twirled around and her features changed instantly. Her long hair retracted and her soft jaw sharpened. Her body morphed until the young woman was gone and a dapper man stood in front of me with his muscled chest on display. With a lower voice, he addressed me. "Or would you prefer if I looked like this, My Queen?"

I opened my mouth to protest but the

shapeshifter was twirling around again, this time transforming into a small child with golden hair and a cheeky grin. "I'll be whoever you want me to be, ruler of the Underworld."

Before Erebus could change again, I held out my hand. "Stop. That's enough. Why don't you take on your own form?"

"My own… form?" The child stared at me like I grew another head.

I nodded. "Yes, that'll do just fine."

The nymph hesitated for a moment before turning again, this time allowing her otherworldly features to shine through. Her pale skin took on a light green hue and thick leaves emerged from her shoulders, wrapping around her as garments. Not quite young, not quite old, her human features mixed flawlessly with her natural look. She looked fierce and yet, insecure to be standing in front of me like this. "Does my appearance please you now, Your Darkness?"

"If you're comfortable, then yes. And just Maia, please."

"Yes, Maia." The nymph pondered for a moment. "You're the first in a while that doesn't have a request for me."

So that was what the fair maiden was about. No doubt the fantasy of my predecessor, who by all accounts, wasn't very competent. None of them were.

"Would you care for a tour?" Erebus asked, growing more confident in her own skin with every passing moment.

"Maybe later. I'm tired from my journey."

"Of course, you are. Please allow me to escort you to your wing and alert the cooks. You must be hungry."

"I'm starving," I admitted, following her into the large hall. "How long have you been here?"

"I've been serving for five hundred years," she replied, her voice swelling with pride.

"Wow. That's amazing. I'll have to rely on your knowledge and wisdom. I'm not quite sure what's expected of me but I'll do my very best."

"Anything you desire, Your Darkness. I am your humble servant." Erebus chattered away about all the other things she wanted to do for me as she showed me to my chambers, her genuine excitement contagious.

A warm welcome in a cold, miserable place.

I contemplated asking her to use my name again but I had a feeling it wasn't going to stick. I'd just have to get used to my new title.

After a whole lot of stairs and long winding halls, we arrived at my wing. Despite all the black iron everywhere, I could tell someone attempted to soften up the features with black woods and marble. It only helped a little. The large four poster bed was the only thing that looked remotely comfortable.

Erebus followed me into the room and placed a small crystal bell on the nightstand. "If you desire anything, small or grand, just ring the bell and we'll attend to you."

I could see how lots of people would abuse that feature but I wasn't looking to be pampered and spoiled. Even if most people were convinced I was a joke and not fit to run this place, I was determined to show them otherwise. I was going to prove to them how capable their new Hades was.

TWO

Maia

My eyes opened up to a foreign ceiling and the smell of new sheets.

Right. I was in the Underworld. I almost forgot.

Carefully, I slid my legs out from under the satin covers and onto the cold floor. A shiver ran up my body and I reached for the black nightgown at the end of the bed. I assumed that was mine.

Technically, everything down here was now mine. From the dark grey mountains to the long, winding river of death, and all the people in it. I couldn't quite grasp the vastness of my new role yet but it was certainly overwhelming to think about the sheer power I now had. *Technically.*

Everyone knew that the Hades was more a figurehead than anything else. A puppet to sit on a throne while others did the heavy lifting. Maybe that was a good thing, I had no real clue what was expected of me anyway.

I stretched the sleep out of my muscles and crossed the room to the large window. Drawing the heavy curtains back, disappointment flashed through me as the view was just as misty and dark as when I arrived. Of course. There was no sunrise here.

What a shame. The gardens were lush with all kinds of plants and bushes I'd never seen before and the blooming fields stretched out all the way to large mountains. I could even see the Styx from here and the ships with souls ferrying across.

What a sight... A good reminder too. I really was in the Underworld.

A knock on the door cut my viewing time short and I froze. Was I supposed to open it? Did I shout? What was appropriate here?

The person knocked again and I finally found my voice. "Come in."

The door swung open and Erebus rolled in a small cart. "Good midnight, Your Darkness."

"Midnight?" I echoed. I thought it was morning. Did I sleep that long?

The nymph smiled. "The days are backwards here. You'll rise at midnight and rest when morning comes. You'll get used to it."

"I see."

"Admiring the view?" she asked, gesturing to the window.

"Yes. It's quite something."

"That it is, Your Darkness."

"Maia," I reminded her gently, gesturing to the cart. "Is that breakfast?"

"Oh, no. Those are supplies for the other rooms and servants. You'll have breakfast in the Grey Hall. Unless you'd prefer to take it up in your chambers?" she said, worry flitting across her features when she realised she might have displeased me.

I quickly reassured her. "No, I'll have breakfast in the Grey Hall. I'd love to see more of the palace. Well, and the rest of the Underworld."

Erebus bowed slightly. "I can give you a tour after your meal and arrange for a guide later, if you wish."

"That sounds wonderful, thank you."

"No need for gratitude, I'm merely your humble servant," she said, her voice quivering slightly.

I ignored it even if I wanted to know what that

was about. It was going to take a while to get used to all the customs down here and I wasn't going to learn them by alienating the person who ran the household.

The nymph retreated from my room, lingering on the threshold. "Shall I send up maids to help you in your garments?"

"Help me with my garments? What, like I'm royalty?" I joked. "Thank you, but I can dress myself."

"Royalty?" Erebus looked insulted. "*Royalty?* Your Darkness, you are *divinity*. A God amongst mortals. Kings and queens bow to you. You're the ruler of the dead, the master of the Underworld."

Her intensity made me uncomfortable. Perhaps all those things were true once, but that was a long time ago.

Not sure what to do, I just smiled awkwardly. "Of course. Well, if it's all the same, I'd prefer to dress myself."

"If that pleases you, Your Darkness," she replied, bowing deeply as she left.

The tension jittered through my legs and I sat back down on the bed, feeling myself relax. Everything was already so much more stressful than I anticipated and I hadn't even started with any of my new duties yet. This was just mundane stuff.

I opened the closet and was greeted with an entire walk-in. The hangers were loaded with all kinds of options and styles. Not sure about the dress code for my daily duties, I selected a rather plain blouse with long sleeves and a pencil skirt that covered my knees.

Hopefully, this would be okay for my first day. Doubt crept in as I got dressed. Maybe I should've had a maid dress me after all.

I examined myself in the mirror and the first hint of doubts crept into my mind. The mousy girl staring back at me wasn't qualified to be here. With my stupid drab hair and my forgettable face, people were never going to take me serious. It just looked like I was playing dress-up in adult clothes, someone that had no clue what they were doing.

I was going to run the Underworld? *Me*? This was a joke. I was a joke. What was I thinking coming down here?

No.

I slapped my own cheeks, trying to dispel the doubts and worrying thoughts. It was too late to turn back so it was useless to question my choice. This was happening and I just had to get on board.

Before my reflection could whisper more negativity in my ear, I turned away from the mirror and abandoned my room so I could get breakfast, like Erebus said. Except I didn't know where the Grey Hall was. Great.

I searched the hallway for Erebus but it was empty. The entire wing was deserted and eerily quiet, not helped by the torches on the wall flickering with blue fire. This place would definitely benefit from a makeover.

"Hello?" I called, but there was no reply. As expected.

Now what? Should I just venture out into the palace and hope I'll find my way?

No, that was foolish. I couldn't even remember how I got from the front door to here, I'd just get lost. That would be embarrassing.

I only had one choice.

Reluctantly, I returned to my room and grabbed the crystal handbell waiting on the nightstand. Like a spoiled princess, I rang the damned thing and immediately, someone knocked on the door.

"Come in," I called, quickly putting the bell down. I hated every moment of that but I had no choice.

The door swung open and instead of Erebus, a tall and slender man in a dark suit waited on the other side. He bowed slightly, revealing the horns on top of his head. "I'm Stephan, your personal aid. What can I do for you, Your Darkness?"

"I'm supposed to have breakfast in the Grey Hall but I don't know where that is."

Stephan nodded and smiled stiffly. "I'll escort you, Your Darkness."

"Please call me Maia," I requested, hoping he will listen. If I was going to make it down here, people needed to stop calling me those silly titles.

The tall man didn't seem too sure but nodded nonetheless. "Whatever you desire, Maia. Please allow me to escort you."

I followed him through the hall, my footsteps and his hooves echoing in the silence. The place was a maze and I was glad that I hadn't gone out by myself. I definitely would have gotten lost.

After what seemed like a thousand steps and a thousand stairs, we finally arrived at the aptly named Grey Hall. Apart from the black table and throne-like seat, everything else was grey. The walls, the decorations, even the paintings. Like someone sucked all the colour out of the room. Not exactly an exciting place to start the day but at least it made the vibrant food waiting on the table even more inviting and tempting.

A servant pulled the throne back for me and I sat down, staring at the mountains of food piled on golden trays. There were all kinds of colourful berries and oddly shaped fruits sitting around large chunks of meat and pies. A roasted bird with four legs sticking up in the air on top of some wilted black leaves served as the centrepiece.

It looked a little frightening so I decided to go for some fruit. There were some strange orange-like things with spikes that looked dangerous to eat so I picked something that looked like a hybrid apple-cucumber. Despite its appearance, it was soft to the touch and burst in my mouth with zingy freshness.

Surprised by the vibrant taste, I devoured it. I didn't expect food down here to taste so lively but then again, plenty of people in the past were seduced by the bounty of the Underworld to the detriment of return.

I froze mid bite and stared up at Stephan, some juice leaking out of my mouth. "This is going to sound silly, but I'm not trapped down here now I've taken a bite, right?"

He smiled reassuringly. "Of course not, Your Darkness. You're the Queen of the Underworld and everything in it. You're not bound by the laws here, you make them. Would you like to visit the Overworld or Mount Olympus? I can ready your carriage."

"No, that's quite alright." Just the thought of that nauseating ride turned my stomach.

I swallowed the bite of whatever fruit I was

eating, hoping Stephan was telling me the truth and I hadn't just doomed myself. It was one thing becoming the new Hades, it was a whole other not being able to return to the land of the living… ever.

Then again, anyone I missed would eventually become my guest so in the grand scheme of things, not that disastrous.

THREE

Maia

Once I finished eating, the servants cleared the table and left me in the Grey Hall without anything to do. With the food removed, the monotonous colour was really boring and drab. Overwhelmingly so.

I sat up to request a change of scenery and like magic, Erebus showed up from nowhere with a big smile on her face. She remained at a respectful distance and bowed deeply. "Was breakfast satisfactory, Your Darkness?"

"It was very nice," I answered, still able to taste the sweetness of the fruit in my mouth.

"Excellent. What would you like to do as your next activity? I could prepare a relaxing bath for you or show you to our wine cellars? A day of hunting? Or perhaps Your Darkness would like some company sent up to your chambers. Men? Women? Both?"

I stared at her. Was this what my predecessors have been doing? Lounging around, being spoiled like kings and queens, passing the days with meaningless activities?

"What about my daily duties?" I inquired, stopping her in the middle of another suggestion.

She exchanged a confused look with Stephan, both looking surprised that I wasn't jumping on the opportunity to get wasted or kill some innocent creatures.

"Your daily duties?" Erebus repeated slowly, like perhaps she misheard me.

"Yes. As the ruler of the Underworld, surely, I have tasks to do and people to oversee?"

"Well, yes."

"I'd like to start on those right away," I decided confidently, rising from my throne. "What is expected of me?"

"Umm. Not much, Your Darkness. There are regular reports that require your signature and occasionally, a permission slip. There's the invite to the annual Olympus ball but rest assured, we take care of the preparations. Oh, and you have a monthly meeting with the Persephone that you have to attend to keep her and their side happy but apart from that, the system and Kleon keep things running."

"Kleon?"

"Your assistant. Have you not met Kleon yet?"

I stared at her. "No."

"He usually introduces himself to the new Hades within the first week. I'm sure he'll show up soon," Stephan offered kindly.

Annoyance flickered through me. If he was my assistant, why was I meeting him on his terms? Not just that, was I not allowed to pick who assisted me instead of the other way around?

It was a miracle the Underworld was still running with all this incompetence. No wonder nobody wanted this position, it was like becoming captain of a sinking ship. Despite having only been for a short while, I could see what a mess this was.

What did I get myself into?

I cleared my throat, trying to embrace the situation. It was too late to go back on my decision and even if I did, that would mean rejoining Hera & Co and all the bullies. I'd rather not.

With a sigh, I rose from my seat. "Do I have an

office or a study or something? I'd like to get familiar with my duties."

Even though she seemed surprised, Erebus nodded and guided me through the palace. After only a short walk, we arrived at a set of tall double doors framed with intricate gold decorations. She opened the office for me and I stepped from the cold blue hallway into an oasis of gold. Bookshelves reached all the way to the high ceiling and were packed with old books and tomes. A large chandelier swung above the desk and cast a warm glow throughout the space, making it feel bigger than it was. Whoever designed this place had taste.

The whole vibe was so different from the rest of the palace and I was all for it. It was actually cosy and felt like a place where I could spend some time.

"Would you like anything else?" Erebus asked from by the door.

"No, thank you. This is perfect."

"Then I'll leave you to it. If you need assistance, just ring the crystal bell," she said, gesturing to the familiar bell on the desk. With a smile, she disappeared.

It was a little strange stepping into an office that was and wasn't mine. I could tell that someone else set it up with a lot of care and attention but I also knew that person was long gone. Whatever they did or left behind, it was mine to keep or change.

I trailed my hand along the large, black desk first and sat down in the chair behind it. The leather shrieked but it was surprisingly comfortable. Much better than the awkward chairs at the dining table.

After rummaging through some of the drawers and cupboards, partly for information, partly because I was curious, it became annoyingly clear there was nothing here to help me figure out what I was supposed to be doing.

I glared at the crystal bell tauntingly sitting on the corner of the desk. Ringing it would be like admitting defeat and acknowledging I was entirely clueless and unprepared. But what other choice did I have?

Reluctantly, I gave it the smallest cling and not even five seconds later, someone knocked on the door.

"Come in!" I agreed, worry flashed through me that I'd be told off for sitting at the desk. I suppressed the silly thought and remained in the chair, drumming my fingers on the wood. I was the Hades, I could sit wherever I wanted.

The doors opened and a short man with glasses and a briefcase strode in. He bowed deeply in front of me and saluted for good measure. "At your service."

"I presume you're Kleon?"

He nodded, adjusting the heavy glasses on his nose. "That's me."

"Oh, great. I could use some help with—" I gestured to everything. "This."

"It would be my honour to assist you."

"Thank you. I'm just not very sure what exactly I'm supposed to do."

He sat down in one of the chairs opposite me and opened his briefcase. "Your Darkness shouldn't worry too much. Your duties are minimal and uncomplicated. The system does most of the work on our side."

"And what about Persephone's side?" I inquired. I thought I ruled over the entire Underworld but it was clear there was a hard divide.

"Yes, she and her minions take care of processing the new souls and ferrying them over the Styx from the Docks to the Harbour."

"That sounds like most of the work," I remarked.

Kleon shook his head. "No, the souls still need to be registered in the Terminal and judged before they pass on. That's our domain."

"I thought the entire Underworld was my domain."

He averted his gaze. "It is, Your Darkness, but I would advise you to work *with* the Persephone. Her position has been part of the Underworld almost as long as yours."

"I've heard the stories. What do you know about their relationship?"

"She was a mighty competent companion. It was no surprise when he gave her as much power as he did and she in turn ruled the Underworld with him and for him. Her successors have certainly solidified their position."

"I see. Well, I have every intention of working with her. Even the land of the dead needs harmony. How about we go over those reports first and perhaps, you can tell me a bit more about the good old days."

The man smiled as he shut his briefcase. "Wonderful. It'll be my honour serving you, Your Darkness."

"Likewise. So what should I do first?"

He handed me a journal. "Probably the monthly meeting. It's in a couple of days and you'll want to make a good impression on Persephone. She, umm…"

"She?"

He chuckled uncomfortably. "Nevermind. You'll find out."

FOUR

Penelope

Most Persephones saw more Hadeses in their career than they could count. Despite it being a position for life, most of the candidates weaselled themselves out after only a couple of years and left us to clean up their mess. And people were surprised why we were known for chaos down here.

Those things didn't fly on my term and the new Hades could get on board or get out of my way. That strategy worked with the last couple of them.

My heels clicked on the stone floor as I strode through the narrow hallway to the monthly meeting. The ceiling swallowed the walls and funnelled me through the large door at the end. The black wood was framed with hard steel and three intimidating stone dog heads hung above the entrance, threatening anyone who dared walk under them.

I turned around to my assistant. "That reminds me. I need to feed Cerberus when I get back. Put that in my diary so I don't forget."

"Yes, Mistress," Molly replied dutifully as she scribbled the memo in my hellfire red journal. The smell of ink woke the snakes in her hair and they curiously descended to the paper, eager for a sniff. "Not now," she grumbled, swatting them away. The snakes hissed but reluctantly entwined into a braid and went back to sleep.

If only my hair cooperated like that.

"I hate meeting a new Hades," I complained as I prepared myself. "They're always so incompetent. Why do they even bother sending candidates down, the Underworld runs fine without them. Well, not fine, but, ugh."

Molly carefully patted me on the back. "I know how much you despise it. It's just one meeting. Just put the new Hades in their place like always and things will be back to normal in a week. Or less."

"I hope so. I have so much to do, these meetings are just a waste of my time." With a sigh, I ran my hands down my long, red dress. I didn't want to lose my patience before I'd even set foot inside.

Already done with this, I knocked on the heavy door and it swung open immediately. A young, mousy woman greeted me at the entrance, nervously tucking her brown hair behind her ears. "You must be the Persephone."

I didn't recognise the new girl but I didn't bother wasting time on introductions. Her obvious statement wasn't worthy of response either, obviously, I was the Persephone.

Annoyed, I marched to the two chaises in the middle of the room and occupied the left one, the same side I'd sat on for the past hundred years. I looked up at the other woman. "Where is the new Hades? They're late."

The woman released a nervous chuckle as she sat down opposite me. "That's me," she said, gesturing to herself with shaky hands. "Nice to meet you. I'm so nervous, it's only my sixth day here. Would you like a beverage?"

Despite my best intentions, I snapped. "I don't have time for beverages. This is an important, serious job and I intend to make the most of my term. Unlike you, I can't just sit around and do nothing for the next century. I'll get voted out."

The woman frowned. "I don't intend to sit around."

"Really? I'll believe it when I see it."

"So you don't have time for beverages but sarcasm is fine?" she returned, her eyebrows raising.

What could have easily been a sarcastic remark back sounded like a genuine question, which only annoyed me even more. I glared at the newcomer, already done with this whole thing. It was better if she just stayed out of my way and let me do my job.

The new Hades studied me with reserved but attentive curiosity. "Are you always like this?"

"Like what?" I bit back.

"Hostile," she commented.

"I'm not hostile, I'm direct and I don't have time for anything else."

"Okay."

Even more frustrated than before, I beckoned for my journal from Molly and the gorgon rushed over and put the leathery book in my grip. I flicked it open, determined to get through this meeting as fast as possible. "First item—"

"Perhaps we could do introductions first?" the other woman said. "We'll be seeing a lot more of each other in the coming years. Why don't I start? I'm—"

I held up my hand, already having heard the

same story from all her predecessors. "Don't bother, I know your type. None of you are ever serious about the position. It's supposed to be lifelong but all your predecessors somehow manage to get out of it after ten-ish years and I doubt you'll be any different. You're just here to waste away time until Zeus allows you to return to whatever position you came from."

The woman across stared at me, her stunned expression confirming I hit the nail on the head.

Why couldn't Zeus ever send me a competent candidate? Working in the Underworld wasn't some temporary job or punishment, to some of us, this was a real job. A good job.

I released an angered breath, trying my best to remain dignified. "The truth is, you're neither motivated nor qualified for this job and you have no intention of doing it either. And you know what? That's fine. The Underworld has been running fine without a Hades at the helm and we'll continue to do so. A word of advice? While you're down here, just stay out of my way." My fingers dug into the soft velvet arms, the annoyance flitting through me like a tumultuous river heading to a waterfall. "Unless you have anything of importance to say, don't disturb me. Oh, and here are the monthly reports from my side. Not that any of you ever bother to look. Well, if that's everything, see you next month."

Without waiting for a reply, I slapped my journal shut and rose from the seat. My assistant quickly joined my side and without another look, I strode to my entrance and left. I didn't have time to babysit another Hades.

FIVE

Penelope

NOT A DAY PASSED in the Underworld that I wasn't needed to put out a fire somewhere. Dressed for success, I made my way through the long hallway, gliding along the golden floor to the front door. The handles twinkled as the old butler opened them for me and I stepped outside into the same old night. I wasn't sure why I kept expecting it to be different. Everything was always the same.

With a sigh, I caught my reflection on the golden floor. Despite the darkness, all the excessive metal shimmered and shone with enough intensity to blind. Anyone new to the Underworld would probably admire the stuff but after a century, I'd seen enough gold for a lifetime.

Typical humans and their insatiable greed. We only asked for a small fare but they kept arriving with as many riches as they could.

Pondering, I stared up at the dark ceiling that doubled as a sky. While it wasn't quite as dark as the nights in the Overworld, there was no beautiful moon or stars to watch over us. And even worse, there was no sunrise. The one thing I missed most from my past life. I'd never feel the gentle warmth of the late afternoon sun on my skin or the blazing heat in summer.

The sacrifices I made for power.

With a deep breath, I made my way down the stairs where my carriage was waiting. Drawn by six black rams and made entirely out of gold, nobody would ever mistake who it belonged to.

After a short ride, my chariot came to a brisk halt at the Terminal where the souls disembarked from their ferries. I climbed out, careful to avoid the deep mud. My heels were not made for that.

The rams trampled their hooves impatiently and raced off as soon as I was out, bleating as they disappeared into the surrounding green mist. Six nymphs greeted me with a bow, each greener and paler than the other. At some point, they probably had been beautiful but almost nobody could withstand the corruption of the Underworld.

"Your Greatness," Molly said, greeting me with a weird, jittery smile on her face.

That was never a good sign.

"Status?" I asked, holding my hand out for the daily file.

Molly handed me a clipboard as she and the other nymphs fell in line, following me closely along the pier. "Your Greatness. Umm... Everything is running as it should but—"

"Did you get the numbers from the Docks?" I interrupted, flipping through the document quickly. As expected, there were all kinds of emergencies and disasters rearing their ugly head. I suppressed a sigh. If only someone did their duty, this wouldn't be nearly as hard.

"Yes, the dead are still arriving faster than we can handle them. Mistress, there's something—"

"How many jumpers so far?" I stared down at the water of the Styx, not pleased by the murky colour. There was nothing worse than human pollution.

"Seventeen, I got the report from Styx's temple earlier. They're not happy with it."

"I'm not happy with it either. Tighten security, I don't want to lose more souls."

Molly nodded hastily. "Will do but there's another matter to address first. You have an unexpected—"

Before she could finish her sentence, I spotted a commotion near one of the bays. Workers were stopping to look at something and seemed distracted by whatever it was. No wonder nothing ever got done around here.

"Someone better tell me what's going on!" I demanded, rushing into the mass. My heels clicked on the wooden planks and the sound warned the workers to get out of my way.

At the centre of the commotion, a familiar figure turned around and waved amicably. "Hello!"

Foam formed in my mouth. What was she doing here? She'd only been in the Underworld for a week and she was already here to criticise me? This better was a joke.

Without any regard for the workers, I stormed through them until I was face to face with the mousy woman. "What's the meaning of this?"

She held up one of my red files and gestured around. "While I went through the reports of last year, I noticed you kept highlighting the Terminal and Harbour as one of the main issues for the overcrowding so I thought I'd come see for myself."

Surprise laced through me, settling the anger. "You... read the reports?"

"Yes, it took me a while to get through them all but I think you're right. I've only seen one ferry unload and the entire process is just chaos. Are there supposed to be so many passengers per ship? That doesn't seem right." She turned to look at one of the many temporary holdings and hummed. "I checked the charts earlier and there are still souls here from last week so why do we have more new arrivals?"

Before I could answer, Molly jumped in with one of her own charts. "Don't blame us. We're bringing people at an accelerated rate across but only because there are massive overcrowdings at the Docks. We have no choice but to ferry them across or there won't be room for new arrivals. We can't have the dead linger at the threshold."

The new Hades nodded. "So you're saying the problem is with how fast my people are processing the new arrivals here at the Terminal?"

My assistant hummed as she looked at me for guidance, her bewildered and confused expression reflecting my own feelings.

"Yes," I snapped, finally finding my voice again. Maybe she took me off guard by showing up here but I wasn't going to let her pass the blame. "The whole process is terribly inefficient and even when we get the souls from the Terminal into Holding, the three judges take way too long deliberating. Sometimes it takes them a whole day to reach a decision. Do you know how many souls arrive in that time?"

"Approximately three-hundred and twelve," Mousy said with a smile. "I read the charts."

"Right."

"So we're in agreement."

I stared at her, not sure if I was hearing things correctly. "We are?"

"Yes. The Terminal and Harbour are clearly problem areas that I need to sort out immediately." She straightened her back as she strode towards one of the loading docks where a ferry was about to board.

I broke out of my stunned demeanour and chased after her, eager to see her response. While I knew my side wasn't running as optimally as it could, there were plenty more issues with her minions. Despite the many flashing lights and signs, the response of the terminal workers was incredibly slow. Most of the agents didn't bother getting up until the ferry had passed through the channel and the ferryman needed to request permission to dock twice.

Throughout the whole process, I expected a barrage of questions and remarks but she watched the entire thing in silence while diligently taking notes. After all the souls were unloaded, she made a final scribble and nodded. "I think I have enough for now. This was very helpful. Thank you. I'll get out of your hair now." She turned around, took a couple of steps, and twirled back around. "Oh and just so you know, I volunteered for the position."

Her remark left me even more stunned than before. In all my years, only a handful of gods and demi-gods had visited willingly but even out of those few, none of them would give up the luxuries of Mount Olympus for the depressing darkness of the Underworld, especially when the Hades position didn't give anyone actual power. So what kind of person would volunteer for the job?

Intriguing.

I still wasn't convinced about my new counterpart but maybe I was judging a book by its cover. Maybe she was different from all those before her.

With a hundred thoughts running through my mind, I looked at my rippled reflection in the murky water of the Styx. I couldn't remember the last time the river was clear and clean. Maybe it was an idle dream but if the new Hades truly proved to be different, maybe there was a chance to restore the Underworld to its former glory.

SIX

MAIA

AFTER BEING the new Hades for a couple of weeks, the growing problems of the Underworld were slowly becoming clear to me. And so did my worries about how to solve them. I'd made grand declarations but how was I going to fulfil them?

And what would happen if I couldn't? Letting our guests down couldn't be a good thing or Penelope wouldn't be so stressed about it all.

With a sigh, I flicked through the latest report, the numbers and words dancing in front of my eyes. I really needed a break but I didn't want to give up yet.

Despite my initial reluctance, I rang the crystal bell and only moments later, someone knocked on the doors of my office.

"Come in."

Erebus stepped in, pulling a little cart behind her with a golden dome. "I've taken the liberty to bring you a snack, Your Darkness."

"That's exactly what I wanted, thank you." I got up from my desk and sat down in the little salon. Erebus plated up the selection of fruit and cheeses on the round table and accompanied it with a bottle of red wine. "Anything else I can do for you?"

I popped an imported grape in my mouth. "No, thank you. Wait, actually. Do you handle matters outside the castle?"

"I'm afraid I don't."

"Hmm. So who is in charge of hiring more staff?"

"That depends on the job. We have separate hiring teams for the Terminal and each of the afterlives. If you want more people at the castle, I'm your girl. But for the Docks, that's Persephone's domain. Clean-up crew for the rivers goes through Styx's temple," she explained.

"I see. So where would I find the hiring team for the Terminal?"

"You can call a meeting with your advisors anytime you desire, you're the Hades."

"Right, of course. I'll do that. Penelope's reports made it very clear that the biggest obstruction issue is due to the inefficiency of the Terminal so if we can hire more people, that should solve that."

Erebus released a funny hum. "If I may give you a word of advice?"

"Please."

"Hiring more staff won't be easy. Not a lot of people want to give up their bliss in Elysium for a thankless job."

I studied her. "Do you think it's a thankless job?"

"Me? No but lots of people see it differently," she quickly denied. She returned to her cart, grabbing it by the handles. "If that's all?"

"Another question. I ran into Penelope earlier and she wasn't exactly friendly. Is she always like this?"

The nymph nodded reluctantly. "She has to be. She's strict and harsh but she was elected unanimously a long time ago and there hasn't been a single motion to replace her in her term. She has to be hard to keep everyone in check."

"Including me," I muttered.

"You'll have to forgive her." Erebus smiled. "She

hasn't had it easy with the eb and flow of the Hadeses."

"You respect her," I realised. "A lot."

She nodded. "We all do. It won't be easy to win her over but I believe the effort will be well worth your time."

I nodded, contemplating how I could foster a good relationship with her. Maybe if I could convince her I wasn't another lazy good-for-nothing, maybe she'd take the time to get to know me and work with me. I just had to impress her.

"Anything else?" Erebus asked.

"No, that's all. Thank you for the food." I sank into the seat, nibbling on the variety of cheeses. Most tasted quite familiar and I assumed they were imported from the Overworld too.

After my meal, I returned to my reports and got through as many as I could. I kept hoping a solution would hit me in the face but besides hiring more staff, there was not much else I could do. And from looking at the latest number of hirings, that was going to be a challenge in itself.

I was so not qualified to tackle all these problems. No wonder my predecessors decided to sit back and do nothing. It didn't help that Penelope hated my guts and yet, I wanted to appease her.

What a mess.

With a sigh, I leaned back into my chair and pushed the files away. Relentlessly staring at them wasn't going to magically solve all my issues. Instead, I should get a good night's sleep.

Once again, I rang the crystal bell and it only took Stephan five seconds before he entered my study.

He bowed. "What can I do for you, Your Darkness?"

"I'm sorry to inconvenience you but I still can't find my way up to my chambers by myself," I admitted, feeling my embarrassment grow. Queen of the Underworld and I got lost in my own palace. How ridiculous was that?

Luckily, the satyr didn't seem to mind. "I'll happily escort you to your wing."

"Thank you, Stephan."

"It's my pleasure to serve you."

He dimmed the lights around the place and with a last look at the taunting files on my desk, I left the ornate study. Of all the places in the castle, this was by far my favourite room.

Stephan escorted me through the dark hallways, his hooves clicking on the stone floors.

Blue light from the torches cast long shadows over us, the atmosphere unnecessarily eerie.

"Why are the torches this colour?" I inquired.

"One of your predecessors thought it gave the place a certain gravitas," Stephan replied. "Do you not like them?"

I shrugged. "Not particularly."

The conversation fell flat and I remained silent, trying to memorise the turns from my office to my chamber. After a couple of hallways and staircases, I broke the silence. "Can I ask you a question, Stephan?"

"Of course, Your Darkness."

"What do you know about the overcrowding? When did it start?"

He thought for a moment. "I believe it's been centuries in the making. A long time ago, when humans believed more, they arrived ready and willing. Now most seem surprised this is all real, they didn't bring the right fee, they don't want to go on the ferry. There's always something to cause delays."

That made sense. If only I had a way to make things run smoother but it wasn't just up to me. I'd have to get Penelope on board as well but she didn't strike me as someone that was easily impressed.

After a maze of hallways, we finally arrived at my chambers. I lingered in the doorway, one more question burning on my mind. "What do you know about the current Persephone?"

"Penelope?" Stephan seemed surprised that I was asking about her. "She's excellent at her job."

"She doesn't seem to like me."

"I don't believe it's personal, Your Darkness."

That somehow made it worse. "If I'm going to be able to do my job here, I'll have to get on her good side but I don't know how. Any ideas?"

The satyr scratched one of his horns. "You could invite her for dinner?"

"Dinner," I muttered, letting the idea percolate. Sometimes the simplest answers were the best ones. "I can do dinner."

"Excellent. I can extend an invitation on your behalf, if you so wish."

"That sounds good. Goodnight." I closed the door to my chambers and leaned against the cold wood.

SEVEN

PENELOPE

ON RARE OCCASIONS, something resembling sunlight graced the Underworld. Not quite as bright, not nearly as warm, but a welcome relief from the eternal twilight.

"I'll have my breakfast on the patio," I told Remus, gesturing to the little table overlooking my luscious gardens.

"Right away," he answered warmly, retreating to instruct the other servants.

Leisurely, I took to my seat and basked in the faint glow. Day and night didn't mean anything down here but I preferred to think of this as the morning. A gentle awakening in the land of the dead where nobody but the living and the peaceful slept.

Remus brought my daily tea and I savoured the bitter smell. It wasn't quite like the Overworld coffee but it was similar enough to do the trick.

Halfway through my cup of tea, Molly appeared from the mansion with an annoyed look on her face.

"Good morning," I said. "What brings you here this early?"

"You've got mail." She held out a black envelope with Hades' official seal. "It's from… her."

I ignored the distaste in her voice and accepted the letter. I didn't receive a lot of post, the Underworld wasn't exactly a popular destination, and certainly not Hades.

"What does it say?" Molly asked, not able to hold her curiosity.

"It's an invitation for dinner. Tonight," I read, touching the handwritten note. I'd expected it to feel more demanding or expectant but it felt like a genuine invite.

"Dinner?" Molly pulled up her nose. "I'll prepare a basket of flowers to accompany your rejection."

"Don't," I blurted out, admiring the elegant lettering on the note again. An image of the new Hades struggling with calligraphy popped in my head and I felt a smile tug my lips up. "Actually, I'll accept the invitation. You can still attach the flowers to my response."

The snakes in Molly's hair hissed. "Are you sure? I thought you hated the new Hades. She's just like all the other incompetent candidates from Olympus. Why are you wasting your time?"

"That's none of your business," I returned calmly. "Just make sure the message gets to her right away."

"Whatever you want, Mistress." She sneered, her tone suggesting she meant exactly the opposite. "Anything else I can help you with?"

I dismissed her with a little wave. I had more important things to worry about than a sarcastic assistant. Regardless of my hopes for the new Hades, the Underworld was still a mess and things needed to keep rolling if there was ever a chance of improvement.

After breakfast, I requested my carriage and drove to the Docks to supervise. On arrival, Molly was waiting for me with the same dissatisfied glare.

"Morning," she grumbled again, holding out my journal. "Your tasks for the day."

"Thank you," I said, walking past her to go to the shore. Immediately, I spotted a conflict at one of the terminals. Two guests fighting over a spot in line.

"Hey, you." I addressed one of the security agents. "Don't just stand there. Separate them."

"R-Right away, Your Greatness," he bumbled, hurrying towards the fight. He stepped in between the two women while another guard ushered them out of the line and to the side.

Despite their best attempts to de-escalate the fight, the two women weren't calming down. One of them clawed at the other's face while the other tried to slap her. Their screeching insults caused plenty of people to stop and stare.

How annoying.

I joined the group and my presence immediately put a stop to the fight. "What's the problem here?"

One of the women bowed deeply. "Persephone."

The other wasn't nearly as revering. She remained upright, her glare filled with disdain. "I'm not supposed to be here."

"I'm afraid the Underworld doesn't make mistakes," I told her as kindly as I could. I knew this type of people, this wasn't going to end peacefully. I turned to Molly, shooting her a knowing look. "You should find Seirios."

My assistant nodded and flitted away to fulfil my request.

I turned my attention back to the defiant woman. "I know this is probably not how you planned your day to go but—"

"You think?" she screeched. "I just bought a new couch. This is so unfair. Send me back."

"That's not possible."

"I know it's possible. You just don't want to. I'm just a nobody, no need to treat me special!"

"We treat everyone the same, I can assure you of that," I said despite fully-well knowing it wouldn't make a difference. People lived by convictions and they very rarely changed in death.

"You're all unfair, greedy, miserable vermin down here," she screeched, fighting to get out of the guard's grip. "I bet you're giving this cow here special treatment because she has her fancy gold earrings. Why does she get to go into the express line and I have to wait longer? Well, I'm sorry I can only afford the bare minimum. Not everyone gets to live a life of luxury."

"Again, we treat everyone the same and that's not an express line, just one that was moving faster." Relief filled me when Molly returned with Seirios and two enforcers in tow. I stepped back to allow them access and they took over for the guards, their grip a little firmer.

"Let go of me!" the woman screamed, her shrill voice ringing in my ears.

"You can rejoin the queue when you're a little calmer." I turned to Seirios. "Thank you."

He nodded, not wasting any words, and pulled her along to one of the time-out huts. The guards dispersed, returning to their posts, leaving me with the other woman.

"My apologies," I offered, hoping to resolve this quickly.

The other woman smiled sadly and reached up to one of her earrings. "They're not even real gold. I don't have anything of value with me, I didn't expect to die today." She touched her mouth. "Looks like they forgot to bury me with a coin too."

I smiled. "Not a problem. You'll want to go in that queue then, that's where we accept alternate payments. Nothing nefarious, anything you've got with you with sentimental value will do."

"Oh." The woman looked a lot brighter suddenly. "I didn't realise that was possible."

"It's a new system I'm trying out."

She bowed deeply. "Thank you."

I watched her join the right line, reassured that she won't have to linger for a hundred years. Maybe it put extra strain on the system but it was worth it. Nobody deserved to be stuck here for that long.

Next to me, Molly shook her head. "You're too soft."

"I'm exactly as soft as I need to be," I returned firmly. "Let's go, there's lots more to do."

The rest of the day passed in the usual way and I was cranky, tired, and frustrated by the time I got back to the mansion. I wanted nothing more than a quiet night in but unfortunately, I'd agreed to meet the new Hades for dinner.

As much as I wanted to cancel, nobody cancelled on Hades.

I picked one of my fancier dresses for the night, the smooth fabric cool against my skin. I selected a necklace with ruby stones and matching earrings to finish my outfit.

I briefly paused as I stared at my reflection in the mirror. Why was I putting in effort to impress the new Hades? If anything, she was supposed to impress me.

Still. That wasn't going to stop me from having. Nice evening. Being the Persephone was a lot of hard work so a night out was just what I needed. Whether I'd be in good company remained to be seen.

EIGHT

Maia

Corridor after corridor, door after door, everything looked the same. I was lost, again.

This was what I got for not wanting to bother Erebus or Stephan. Why was the palace a maze? What was the point? To deter guests? Thieves? Bandits? Of all the annoying things in the Underworld, this was by far one of the worst.

After a long day in my study or out at the Terminal, I just wanted to come home and take a nap in bed. Not run a marathon of stairs through the palace in search of my chambers. And to make matters worse, Penelope was going to arrive any moment and I wanted to greet her personally and make a good impression.

A crooked torch looked familiar and I turned left, relieved to find a set of stairs going down. I raced through the hallway, glad to find a familiar turn at the end. I made it.

Panting, I burst into the entrance hall and almost ran straight into Penelope herself.

"I'm so sorry," I panted, trying to steady my breathing. "I got lost, this place is a maze. Sorry."

Her gaze travelled down my body and a bemused smile tugged her lips up. "You alright there?"

"Yes, I got lost on my way down. I must have taken a wrong turn somewhere but I finally made it. Did you know it takes twelve sets of stairs just to get from my wing to here?"

She raised a perfectly shaped eyebrow. "How would I know?"

"Ah. Sorry. Anyway, thank you so much for accepting my invitation." Finally in control of my breathing, I extended my hand. "Let's try introducing ourselves again. I'm Maia, it's nice to meet you."

The other woman stepped forward, taking my hand in hers. She squeezed softly, her grip firm but gentle at the same time. "Hello, *Maia*."

The way she said my name sent a shiver down my spine. It was so deliberate, so intense. Intimidating but intriguing.

Still holding my hand, she gave it a slight shake. "Penelope. You have my apologies for my initial rudeness. It was bad manners on my pat and it won't happen again." Her eyes smouldered, making it clear she meant what she just said.

I smiled, eager to try out her name. "Penelope. I look forward to getting to know you better."

"Me too. The Underworld would greatly benefit from a good work relationship between the Hades and the Persephone."

Right. I almost forgot what this was all about.

She finally released my hand back but I could still feel her touch on my skin. Not wanting to make the same mistake twice, I rang one of the crystal bells by the door.

Stephan appeared from nowhere with a golden tray. "Dinner awaits you, Your Darkness." He bowed slightly towards Penelope. "Your Greatness."

"Your Greatness," I repeated as we followed him. "That's how they address you down here?"

Penelope's lips pursed, her smile evaporating. "Some do."

"Lucky," I grumbled. "I keep asking the staff to

call me Maia but they keep falling back to 'Your Darkness'. What does that even mean?"

Penelope snorted uncharacteristically. Her shocked, horrified look revealed she hadn't meant to laugh and she quickly composed herself, but I knew what I saw. A knowing grin curled my lips up. So underneath that stoic demeanour, there was a sense of humour somewhere.

"After you," I offered as we arrived at the Grey Hall.

Penelope entered the room, pausing hesitantly at the large banquet table. Laden with an abundance of dishes and variety, it looked like a dinner for a small party, not two people. The cooks certainly went all out.

Two plates were waiting on opposite ends of the table and I sat down, disappearing behind a mountain of food. A golden bird in the middle obstructed my view of my guest and made it impossible to converse.

This was even worse than an awkward date. Not that this was one. This was just me getting to know the other ruler of the Underworld over a business meal. Nothing more, nothing less.

Not sure how to even get started on the food, I looked for Stephan but he and all the other servants were already gone. I assumed they'd disappeared to give us privacy but this wasn't making things better.

Not wanting to be spoiled or awkward, I decided not to call them back.

"Help yourself?" I said, gesturing to the sea of food.

Penelope rose from her seat, golden plate in hand. "How are you adjusting to the bounty of the Underworld?"

"I'm getting there," I said, scooping some wilted vegetables on my plate. "Some of the fruit is familiar but all the poultry and fish are very different."

"I remember when I got here. It took me a while to get used to it. However, you can always import goods from the Overworld, if you wish." She loaded her plate methodically, moving along the table to get a little of everything.

"Do you import anything?"

She smiled at me, but it didn't quite reach her eyes. "Only the Hades has that power."

"Ah." I followed suit, eventually meeting her in the middle. "Anything you miss in particular?"

"Coffee. But I'm quite used to the Underworld's delicacies by now." The other woman stood slightly taller than me, her gaze mysterious but warm. "If you need any help with the food, I'd be happy to assist."

"I might take you up on that offer," I smiled, admiring her silently. She was quietly confident and it showed. Not wanting to stare at the beautiful but intimidating woman, I deposited some random meat on my plate and returned to my seat.

Penelope seemed bemused by my nervousness but she was gracious enough not to comment on it. She sat down on the other end of the table, not bothered by the lavish feast in the middle. Perhaps she was used to it.

We ate in silence, prohibited by the distance to make conversation. With every bite, my frustration grew. If I wanted things to be awkward, I would have just gone to one of our monthly meetings.

It was a relief when both our plates were empty and the servants cleared them away. Before Stephan could suggest dessert, I rose from my seat.

Penelope quickly followed suit, giving me a rare glimpse into how she regarded me. Even if she disliked the Hadeses greatly, she still held respect for the position.

"Would you like a drink in my study?" I suggested, not wanting the night to end like this. This dinner was supposed to improve our relationship and it definitely hadn't done that.

Penelope subtly glanced at the thin watch on her wrist and nodded. "I won't say no to one drink."

"Excellent." I felt myself smile. I gestured to the doors, happy to lead her to my office. I smiled at Stephan waiting in the hallway, hoping he wasn't going to take the next thing I said as an insult. "You and the rest of the staff can take the night off."

Surprise flitted through his eyes as he bowed slightly, his pristine dark suit barely wrinkling. "Thank you, Your Darkness."

He sounded genuinely grateful but I made a mental note to check with Erebus what the holiday policies were for this place. The last thing I wanted was to insult any of them.

With Stephan retired for the night, I escorted Penelope to the study personally. The one place in the palace I was confident in finding. Still, I was relieved when we reached it without getting lost.

I pushed the double doors open, stepping aside. "After you."

"Thank you." Penelope crossed into the study, her gaze immediately drawn to the wall of books. "Wow, this is beautiful."

"It's my favourite room in the palace," I admitted, joining her in her admiration. It would take me a good while to read everything in here but luckily, I had eternity to familiarise myself with it all. I gestured to the cosy seating area where I usually have my lunch. "Please."

My guest settled in one of the chairs with a type of grace and authority I could only dream of. The way she was sitting made her chair look like a throne and her like the most powerful woman. She radiated power regardless of what she did. The way she stood, walked, sat. She didn't just wield her power, she was powerful. Like she was born to do this.

A little smirk appeared around the corner of her mouth when she realised I was staring. I quickly averted my gaze and strode to the nearby cabinet to grab two golden chalices, an attempt to hide my fascination with her.

I returned, pretending I couldn't feel her burning gaze on me. "Wine?"

NINE

Maia

I selected a bottle of wine at random, picking one with a nice etiquette and a golden cage around the cork. I fumbled opening it, acutely aware that Penelope was watching my every move. After an awkward struggle, I poured us each a glass, the dark red wine trailing down the sides of the golden goblets.

"There you go." I handed Penelope her chalice, our fingers briefly brushing against each other. I quickly sat down, desperately pretending I hadn't noticed the little spark jumping across.

She smiled knowingly. "Thank you. To our health?"

"To our health," I returned the toast, clinking my cup against hers before taking my first sip. A sour taste coated my tongue and despite its velvety feel, the wine's flavour didn't match the mouth feel.

Penelope almost managed to hide her dislike. "Hmm… That's an… *interesting* flavour."

"Don't drink that, that's awful. Sorry." I grimaced, setting my cup down. "And about dinner too."

"No apology necessary, the food was perfectly fine." She examined the bottle of wine and hummed. "Ah, yes, this is quite an acquired taste. There are plenty of Underworld wines that are a bit easier to drink."

"I don't know much about wine. I never drank it in the Overworld either." I gestured to the cabinet. "Maybe you should select something."

Penelope chuckled as she rose from her seat with feline elegance. "I will. Tell me about your preferences. Sweet or dry?"

"Sweet."

She hummed, examining the bottles. "Do you like adventures or sticking to what's familiar?"

"Are we still talking about wine?"

The other woman looked back at me, her smile growing. "Maybe."

"Well, I'm here so I suppose adventure."

"Fair." She held my gaze, her eyes twinkling. "Easy to consume or do you prefer to savour things?"

"Savour things," I returned, slightly breathless. She was looking at me with such intensity, my chest burned. I'd never had anyone stare at me with this much attention and focus, like she was really trying to see me.

"Me too." She selected a bottle and brought two other chalices back with her. With much more skill than me, she uncorked the bottle and poured the new wine. "Here. If this isn't to your taste, you can always order Overworld wine."

I accepted the cup. "Won't I offend anyone by not adjusting to the tastes of the Underworld?"

"So what if you do? You're Hades, you can do whatever you want." She gestured to my goblet. "What do you think?"

I took a sip, deliberately savouring the flavour. "Mmm. Much better. Lighter, sweeter. I much prefer that."

"Looks like I picked well then," she remarked, drinking too. "Yes, very nice. I prefer it too."

"I'm glad. Sorry about dinner again. The seating

was awkward, wasn't it? When I invited you for dinner, I wanted a nice casual meal where we could talk and get to know each other better. Why is it like the Regency down here? I expected… well… Ancient Greece but it's just a bit of everything."

Penelope shifted in her chair, her smile bemused. "Not even the Underworld is immune to the influence of time and trends."

"Fascinating. How long have you been here again?"

"This is my first term. I started almost a hundred years ago."

"Wow, that's a while. When does your term end?"

"We hold elections every quarter of a millennium. Unlike your position." She took another sip of her wine and looked at me over the rim with piercing eyes. "Tell me, what kind of person volunteers to become the ruler of the dead?"

I let Penelope's question linger for a moment. I expected her to ask, that was all people had been asking me since I accepted the position. I contemplated giving her a vague answer like I gave to most, but there was something about the way she was looking at me that made me feel like I could tell her the truth.

"I was stuck working at Hera & Co. I don't want

to go into detail but some of the people were really awful to me. At the beginning, it was small stuff, too petty to report. When they realised I wasn't going to stand up to them, it got worse but I thought I could endure it. I put in so many requests to transfer but they never got approved. Then one day things just kind of escalated. I don't want to get into it, I—" My voice hitched as the emotions of that day washed over me.

Penelope stayed quiet but I could tell she was listening intently, waiting for the rest of my story.

Grateful for her patience, I took some big gulps of wine, relishing in the stinging taste. "Anyway. I was recovering when I heard of the vacancy. I just signed up on a whim. I didn't think I would actually get it but only days later, I got an official congratulatory letter from the Zeus and there was a carriage with black horses waiting for me. You know the rest."

Penelope released a long breath. "I'm sorry."

"Thank you." Another silence fell over us and I downed my cup in a way to bridge the awkwardness. I gave the bottle a suggestive shake. "More wine?"

"So much more wine," Penelope agreed.

I topped up our goblets and continued drinking, eager to let the warm glow take the sharp edges off of my brain. The soft haze elevated the heavy mood and I gestured to the other woman. "Can I ask you something?"

"Go for it."

"I know I'm new to this role but I want to work with you." I sat up straighter. "If I'm doing something that frustrates you, please tell me instead of going on a little rant."

Penelope chuckled softly. "I did do that, didn't I?"

"Yeah, you did. I get that you hold a lot of irritation towards the previous Hadeses but don't take it out on me."

"It won't happen again," she promised, raising her glass.

We emptied the bottle and then another. The alcohol wasn't quite having the same effect as I remembered from Dionysus' wine but it was definitely creating a buzz.

The more I drank, the more I looked at the woman in front of me. She was so regal and competent, it was admirable. Her confidence shone through in everything she did, even if she was just sitting in a chair and drinking from a chalice.

She noticed me looking, her eyes slightly hazy from all the alcohol. "Are you looking at me?"

"I am," I heard myself admitting.

"Why?"

"You're very beautiful."

Her lips tugged up into a rare but slightly confused smile. "Thank you."

Something about my look must have given away more than I intended. Understanding dawned on her face and her cheeks flushed pink, although that could've been from the wine. "Forgive me if I'm interpreting this wrong but... Are you coming onto me?"

"No, no, no, no. I'm not. I mean, you're my type but that would be a terrible idea. We have to work together and we're just getting to know each other." I rambled, every sentence leaving my mouth faster than the last. "Besides, I'm not looking for romance and I'm sure you're not either, right?"

Penelope remained suspiciously quiet, looking a little embarrassed. Somehow, we found ourselves entangled in a conversation that was too intimate for either of us. A loaded silence hung between us and neither seemed to know how to bridge it.

Slowly, the other woman put her cup down. "I think I should go. It's getting late and we have lots of work tomorrow." She rose from her chair, looking a little taken aback. Maybe even taken off guard.

"Yes, that's probably best. Rulers of the Underworld and all. We shouldn't be hungover," I chuckled awkwardly, trying to dispel some of the sudden tension.

"We shouldn't." She returned a smile. "But I had a lovely evening."

"Me too. We should totally do it again."

"We should," she answered, but I couldn't tell if she meant it or if it was just one of these things people said.

I managed to lead her back to the front door without getting lost in the maze. To be a good host, I opened the heavy doors for her and a gust of fresh air cleared some of the fog in my brain.

"Thank you for the invitation," Penelope said as she stepped out into the clear night, her voice slightly softer than usual. That was probably the wine.

"Thank you for coming. I'm glad we got to know each other better. Because of work. Not like a date. Work."

What was I saying? I needed to gain Penelope's respect and convince her I was a competent woman. All these drunk ramblings were just going to do the opposite. Damn that treacherous wine. It hit me harder than I thought.

"Well, you'll be happy to know I'm slightly more looking forward to working with you." For a moment, she gazed at the misty sky, a mysterious but bitter smile playing around her lips. She took it all in and sighed deeply.

I looked up too. "There are no stars."

"No, but it's still beautiful."

"It is," I agreed. "Do you need a ride? I can get my carriage to drive you home although I wouldn't recommend it. The driver is reckless."

She chuckled. "No, I think the walk will be nice. Good night, Maia."

With a last smile, she disappeared into the night and I watched her leave. Whether I wanted to admit it or not, I was intrigued.

TEN

Penelope

THE COOL AIR was a welcome change from the charged atmosphere in the palace. What was that between Maia and I? Despite her denial, I was almost sure she was flirting with me. Maybe unintentional but the tension... The tension never lied.

Not that it mattered. It would be extremely unprofessional to engage with Maia in any other capacity than colleagues. That being said, I couldn't remember the last time I met someone that intrigued me like her. There was definitely more to her than I initially thought and I felt the temptation to spend more time with her.

Which was exactly what I couldn't allow to happen.

I savoured the thoughts on my walk home but put them out of my head as soon as I arrived at my mansion. My heels echoed sharply on the golden stairs, no doubt alerting my staff to my arrival. As expected, the doors swung open for me and Remus escorted me in.

"Did you have a good evening, Your Greatness?"

"I did," I replied, surprising myself.

"Good. Can I get you anything?"

"No, I'm good. You can retire for the night."

He bowed and disappeared, leaving me on my own in my massive mansion. The place was quiet and empty without the bustling of the staff, something that didn't usually bother me. But after the lively night with Maia, the solitude wasn't as welcome as usual.

I ventured further into the mansion and a light flicked on in the salon. "Mistress."

"Molly. What are you doing here?" I questioned.

My assistant rose from her chair, her eyes dark and desperate. "Waiting for you, of course. It's late. Dinner must have been nice?"

I could easily tell from her sharp tone what she was actually asking. The jealousy and possessiveness weren't hard to spot, especially when all the snakes in her hair were hissing at me.

Not in the mood, I sighed. "Don't start."

"Start what? I'm merely asking how your evening was." She pushed her bottom lip out in a dramatic pout, a trick my younger self fell for many times. But that was then and this was now.

With a shrug, I discarded my purse on the table. "I had a nice evening. How about you?"

"I tapped my snakes for poison and I watched the latest episode of Aphrodite's Golden Apple. I adore watching people find true love. If only I was still alive so I could be on it. Why don't we have an Underworld version of it?"

"Because people aren't supposed to linger here."

Molly scoffed. "And yet, the system would collapse if we didn't linger and work for you."

"If you didn't linger, we wouldn't need a system." I massaged my temples. "Can you leave? I think I've got a headache coming on."

The other woman studied me. "Are you drunk?"

"I might have had a drink or two, not that that's any of your business. Anyway, it's late. I'm going to bed," I announced, hoping to avoid a spat. I wasn't in the mood for a fight and most of all, I didn't owe

Molly an explanation or anything else for that matter.

"Perhaps you'd like company?" the woman suggested, her voice low and sultry. She dragged her hands over her body and pulled some of her skirt up, exposing tempting skin. "I know a way to get rid of that headache of yours."

"Molly," I warned her. "We agreed to keep things professional."

"That's what you said last time in the gardens. And the time before in the study. And the time before that," she whispered while approaching, lust in every flick of her hips.

The rapid change in her mood amplified my headache. I stepped back, not wanting to engage. "I'm going to bed. *Alone*."

"Fine!" Molly screeched, rushing past me on her way out. "I can tell when I'm not wanted. Good luck doing the reports in the morning by yourself!"

"You can't just skip work because I won't have sex with you," I called after her.

"Then I quit!"

"Okay, shall I arrange transport to the Terminal?"

Molly snapped around and her snakes spat poison towards me. "Fuck you."

Unperturbed, I stepped out of reach. "It's a genuine question."

"We both know it's not."

"Then stop threatening you're going to quit."

"Fine. Then… Then… Then I'm taking a holiday. With paid leave!"

"Sure." I shrugged. By now, she should know she couldn't emotionally blackmail me into doing what she wanted. Deeming the conversation over, I retreated to my chambers without wasting another word on her. Despite the little theatrics now, I had a great evening with Maia and I wasn't going to let her ruin that.

I stripped my dress off and curled into bed, savouring the events of the night. In all my years as the Persephone, I didn't expect to come across a Hades I didn't loath and yet, here she was. New, inexperienced, unqualified, but with a lot of promise. This could change everything.

ELEVEN

Maia

Despite not having to see Penelope for a while, I still felt embarrassed about how I conducted myself during our evening. The awkward dinner aside, flirting with her was a real faux-pas on my part. I should've kept a clear head but the Underworld wine really took me off guard.

"How angry would Penelope be if I didn't show up to the meeting?" I asked Stephan as I exited the palace.

"I'm not sure but I would advise against it," he said politely.

I feared as much.

The sound of impatient hooves announced the arrival of my carriage. Foaming at the mouth, the four black horses bristled as the driver kept them in check. He hopped down to open the door for me, bowing so deep his nose touched his knees.

I smiled at him. "Thank you. Any chance we might ride at a... more leisurely speed?" I inquired, hoping my request wasn't unreasonable. It wasn't that I didn't like riding in a carriage, I just preferred my organs to stay in the right place in my body.

Without speaking a single word, the driver nodded and tipped his head, returning to his seat in the front.

"Is he okay?" I asked Stephan, worried I insulted him.

"Yes. He has no tongue," he informed me quietly. "He arrived that way. Nobody knows why but he has his ways of showing his displeasure so don't worry."

"I see. Thank you." At least, it had nothing to do with me. That was somewhat reassuring, but also tragic. I wouldn't want to go an eternity without being able to speak.

I climbed in the carriage and Stephan joined me on the bench on the other side. As soon as I was seated, we shot in motion and my stomach instantly turned despite us going slower than before. Maybe I just wasn't made for horse-drawn chariots.

"Why are the monthly meetings held in the temple? Isn't there a room in the palace that we can use?" I asked, hoping to distract myself from the rising nausea.

Stephan tapped his chin. "The monthly briefings used to be held at the palace but one of the past Persephones made a motion to hold it in the middle, on neutral ground."

What a shame. I'd have to get used to this awful ride then. Or maybe I could walk next time.

We arrived not a second too late at the temple and I tumbled out of the carriage, eager for steady ground under my feet. The driver held up a thumb questioningly and despite the awful ride, I smiled and nodded. "Good, but maybe a little slower next time. But it was good, thank you."

My approval brought a sparkle to his eyes and with the biggest smile, he whipped the horses into motion and sped off.

I gathered a breath stretching the tension out of my muscles and shaking the dizziness away. My stomach still felt like it was tied in a knot but at least I was no longer at risk of vomiting. That was something.

Doing my best to maintain a professional

composure, I made my way into the temple and to the meeting room. In spite of arriving ten minutes early, Penelope was already waiting for me in her chair looking flawless like usual.

I sat down in my seat and conjured a smile. "Penelope."

She returned a polite smile of her own. "Maia. How are you today?"

"I'm well, thank you." I gestured to the empty space behind her. "No assistant?"

"No. Molly is taking a little holiday."

"I see." So holiday *was* a thing here. I definitely had to make sure to discuss this with Erebus so my staff were getting the appropriate days off. I didn't come down here to take advantage of the dead.

"Are you sure you're okay?" Penelope asked, studying at me with sharp eyes.

"Truth be told, I'm a little embarrassed about, you know, the other night," I admitted. I wish I was stronger and didn't feel this way but at least now that I'd confessed, I wouldn't have to hide how horrible I felt. It wasn't like I'd have been able to keep up the ruse anyway.

A slight chuckle escaped the woman opposite of me. "There's no need."

"There is. I shouldn't have made a pass at you, that was incredibly unprofessional of me."

Penelope's eyes flickered. "You didn't, you gave me a genuine compliment and that was it."

"Hmm. Maybe."

"Are you saying it wasn't genuine?" she teased.

"I thought you didn't like wasting time," I echoed her words back from our first meeting in an attempt to change the topic.

She threw her head back and laughed. "Fair enough. Let's just blame the wine."

"I'd like that. It was the wine's fault. Especially that awful first bottle."

"Yes, that was horrendous. Next time, I'm selecting all of the wines."

Next time.

A warm glow spread through me and I found myself smiling from ear to ear. "Sounds good to me."

"I'm only teasing. When I first got here, I ordered some truly awful wines that were ten times worse. I've found some that are more to my taste since though. We have a really rich red that's delicious after dinner."

"Perhaps I should come sample some of that rich red," I blurted out.

Before I could explain that I wasn't inviting myself over for dinner, Penelope spoke. "Maybe you should." She flipped through the red journal on her lap and clicked her pen. "Shall we move onto our reports? We do have an Underworld to run."

I almost forgot that was why we were here. Not that I was ever going to admit that. Determined not to look like a fool, I handed her the numbers for the week from my briefcase.

Penelope stared at the report and back at me like I grew a second head. "What's that?"

"My report. You just said—"

"I'm sorry, you're the first Hades in fifty years to bring a report to the meeting."

I stared at her. "Really? Then what have you been doing all this time to get the statistics from our side?"

Penelope hesitantly accepted the file, still looking in awe. "I send Molly directly to your clerk once a month."

"Wow. Well, that's going to be different from now on," I assured her, pleased I'd managed to impress.

She released an appreciative hum which only added to the sense of validation. I was definitely doing something right. If I could win her over, maybe I wasn't a lost cause as I feared after all.

She caught me smiling and raised one eyebrow. "Yes?"

"Nothing. Do you have a report for me?"

"I do." She handed me a folder from her purse.

"Isn't it funny that someone is printing these for us?" I remarked, accepting the sheets.

"I've never thought about it like that but yes, it is kind of funny." She settled into her chair, looking a lot more relaxed and comfortable than our very first meeting.

A twinge of satisfaction passed through me. I was definitely doing something right.

TWELVE

Maia

It was strange how quickly the Underworld was starting to feel like home. There were still some things I needed to get used to but I was getting the hang of it. It helped that all the staff was competent and seemed happy to work with me.

"Erebus." I smiled at the manager of the palace. "Can I ask you something?"

"Naturally," the nymph replied, pausing on the other side of my desk.

"How easy is it to import things from the Overworld?"

"You merely have to ask."

"Really? And I can have anything I want?"

She nodded. "Anything you desire. If you let me know, I'll make sure to order it for you."

"Great. I'd like a packet of coffee."

"Coffee?" she echoed, seemingly surprised by my request. "Alright. Any particular kind?"

I shook my head. "Just not the cheap stuff, something nice and dark."

"And how much would you like? A year's worth?"

"No, no, just one packet. It's a gift," I told her, closing the report I was going through. "I'm stiff, I think I need to stretch my legs."

"The orchards are particularly nice this time of year," Erebus suggested as we exited my office. "I'll find someone to escort you."

"I prefer to walk next to the Styx," I told her. "And no need, I can go by myself."

"As you wish." She handed me my coat and opened the large front doors, waving me out. "Have a nice walk, Your Darkness."

With a bemused smile, I crossed through the large front gardens, admiring the lustrous variety. I always imagined this place as destitute and dark, but there was a lot of beauty to be found. I just had to know where to look.

It didn't take long to reach the Styx and I

followed the murky river, watching the green water play with the banks. It smelled fouler than I remembered, not quite the relaxing walk I hoped for.

The ground vibrated and a golden carriage flew past me, leaving a plume of dust in its wake. The chariot stopped abruptly and a slender woman stepped out. "Hello."

I raised a hand. "Penelope."

"What are you doing here?"

"I'm clearing my head. Too many reports."

"Ah yes." She joined me by the river, a curious look gracing her features as she examined me. "Would you like some company?"

I gestured to her carriage. "Are you not doing anything?"

"Nothing that can't wait." She nudged me along. "Let's find somewhere nicer to walk where the stench of the Styx won't bother us."

"Please. What's that smell anyway?"

"Rotting souls at the bottom," she replied casually. "Sometimes people jump, hoping to escape their fate."

"Grim."

"It's an issue we're working on but the current Styx isn't exactly bothered. He's also become a bit complacent after all this time. You might want to have a word with him." She gestured up to one of the paths leading into the hills. "This way, I want to show you something."

In companionable silence, we climbed the hill. The fields around us stretched far in every direction and some of them were covered in trellises and vines.

"Grapes," Penelope pointed out. "To make that crappy wine of yours."

I snorted as we continued on. I wasn't sure what we were doing but I was eager to explore the Underworld a bit more, especially with Penelope as my guide.

We passed a field where a bunch of nymphs were planting seeds in the dirt. They paused their work as they saw us and bowed deeply, not looking up until we were past.

"It feels so weird when people bow to me," I admitted, glancing back at the hard workers who were whispering to each other, no doubt about us. If I understood things correctly, it wasn't often that the Hades and Persephone were seen together. Not like this anyway.

"You'll get used to it. Eventually," Penelope replied, her breathing shallowing as we reached the top of the hill.

The green landscape stretched out from under

us and joined together to form the banks of the river of the dead. The large body of water swirled through the land, murky and green, with a steady stream of ships floating along as they carried the dead through the Underworld. The ferries attracted flocks of strange birds with four legs that I'd only seen presented as food so far. They circled around the fleet of ships, carried by the thick mist that hung everywhere. A strangely beautiful sight. Haunting. But beautiful nonetheless.

I gathered a breath. "What a sight."

"Hmm. It never gets old," Penelope agreed, smoothing out her dress. "How does the sun compare?"

"Well, there's not really any sun here, is there?" I stared up at the gloomy ceiling. "This is an illusion right? Who's in charge of it?"

Penelope released a snort. "It's the weather, nobody controls it although I'm sure you could if you put your efforts to it. You're in charge of everything, Maia." She teased, nudging me gently. "*Hades.*"

"No, it's weird when you call me that."

"Oh, my apologies, *Your Darkness.*"

I gave her a teasing shove. "No, stop, stop, that's even worse."

Penelope's genuine laughter cackled over the hills and I joined in, surprised by how easy it was to be around her. The rumours about her had me believing she was hard and cold and intimidating. But standing here, in the faint glow of the Underworld, she didn't look like that at all. She was approachable and warm, and I wanted to do all kinds of things that were definitely not part of my job description.

"Shall we keep walking?" I proposed before I did or said something stupid.

"Yes. Have you seen the Grove? It's where all the grievances and curses of the Overworld manifest. If you're ever looking to run into other deities, that's where you can meet them," she explained as we set in motion, wandering along the path.

"Wouldn't I just see them during the monthly Olympus meeting?"

"Right, you can leave. Ruler and all," she said, her smile hiding a sadness in her voice.

We continued our walk down the hill, the vast landscape stretching out around us. It was serene despite the subtext of death. Maybe it was different to be here, alive, able to return to the Overworld without being chained here for eternity.

I glanced at Penelope, only just realising how clear her skin was. She was untouched by the corruption despite being here for such a long time.

"Do you miss it?" I asked, looking at her curiously.

"Do I miss it? The Overworld? I—" Penelope shrugged, temporarily lost for words.

I spotted a figure crouching down by the river and I grasped her arm, interrupting her. "Shit, I think we've got a jumper! We've got to help."

She held me back. "No, no, that's Hecate. She comes down here every night to bless her talismans and process her curses."

"Oh, I didn't realise." I stared at where her hand was touching me, relishing in her touch. Her grip was gentle but firm. Intentional. I wanted more of it, even if it was a terrible idea.

I quickly stepped back, breaking contact. If there was one person I had to keep my composure around, it was her. Penelope. Persephone. Queen of the Underworld and the one person I needed to foster a good working relationship with. I couldn't mess this up or complicate it with silly feelings or fleeting desires.

Instead, I observed Hecate by the water. A group of dogs had surrounded her and seemed to be helping in some capacity.

"I didn't realise we had those here," I said, pointing at the brigade of canines.

"They're from the Overworld. They collect talismans offered to Hecate and she blesses them here, in the Styx."

"Sounds like a lot of work. She does that all night by herself?"

Penelope sighed. "Yes, I've told her many times she should find people to help her but Despina can be a little set in her ways."

"Should we say hello?"

"No, better not. She prefers keeping to herself." Penelope pensively stared at the woman by the river. "Actually, I might go down and see how she is. We're old friends."

"Right. I should get back to work anyway. I abandoned my reports but I want to have them ready for our next meeting."

A brief smile graced Penelope's lips. "Well, don't let me keep you. I'll see you at our meeting. Good luck with your reports."

"Thanks, let's hope I don't lose my sanity."

"Well, if you ever need a break, you can always stop by the mansion to sample the rich red."

"Right. The wine. At your mansion. I just might take you up on that offer," I replied. Part of me was convinced it was a bad idea but I pushed it away. It wasn't a date, just me getting to know my counterpart. She was the Persephone after all.

THIRTEEN

PENELOPE

I STARED OUT THE WINDOW, watching the green mist in the starless sky. It was beautiful in its own way but it definitely didn't compare to the real thing.

"Your Greatness." Remus bowed slightly as he appeared in the salon. "You have a visitor."

"A visitor? I don't think I'm expecting anyone and I'm tired." I retreated from the window, smoothing out my dress. "I'm going to bed so please tell them to come back another time."

He hesitated, not moving a muscle. "It's… Hades."

"Maia is here?" I froze in my step, immediately perking up. "Well, what are you still doing here? Let her in."

"Are you sure? You said you were tired… I can send her away," Remus offered.

"No, it's Hades. Let her in. No, I'll let her in," I scoffed, waltzing past him to the entrance hall. I hadn't expected her to take me up on the offer for wine but I couldn't say I was disappointed she was here.

I quickly checked my reflection in the golden wall, flattening my hair. For once, the multitude of mirrors came in handy.

With my most charming smile, I opened the door, ready to welcome in Maia. "Welcome to my humble abode," I announced jovially, not sure why I was feeling nervous. I'd never cared what any of the Hadeses thought of me and I wasn't going to start now.

Maia entered and her mouth fell open at all the gold. "Oh my. It's very…" She paused, clearly searching for the right word. "Shiny."

I chuckled at her dry comment. "It is rather. I can't go anywhere without seeing my reflection."

"But it's a good reflection," she quipped, her gaze locked on the golden tiles and our reflection in them.

"Flatterer," I returned with a little eye roll. Even so, I could tell she meant it and that made it worse. She shouldn't be looking at me like that. I shouldn't be either.

"Would you like a tour?" I proposed, gesturing to nothing in particular. I promised her a drink but it felt a little odd to just break out the bottles. We weren't teenagers anymore.

A little smile appeared around Maia's lips. "Please. I heard you have some very nice gardens."

I hoped that wasn't meant as a double entendre. If it was, I wasn't going to act on it. With a polite smile, I gestured towards the patio. "Let's start there then."

The genuine smile stretching across her face when she saw the garden told me it hadn't been a suggestive insinuation and some of the tightness in my chest released. I held the door open for her, regretting it the moment she walked past me and her light perfume captured me.

I followed her out, relieved when the smell of the closing flowers took over. Maia brushed her hands through the leaves as we moved through the gardens, her face bright with awe. We came to a natural halt and she gently touched a flowering bud. "I've always been a fan of flowers but I never imagined there would be so many here. And they're all so colourful."

She was right. The vegetation was surprisingly plentiful and bountiful for a land that welcomed the dead but I'd never looked at it that way. "You're very upbeat for someone that lives in the Underworld," I remarked, surprised by how much I liked her company. "You look like you enjoy yourself."

She smiled at me. "Why wouldn't I? I chose to be here and I'm not dead. Oops. Sorry, if that was insensitive."

"Why would it be? I'm not dead either," I told her, surprising myself that I was freely admitting it.

"Ah right, it's only the river deities that are dead. I forgot." She leaned on the balustrade overlooking the rest of the grounds and turned to me, curiosity playing in her brown eyes. "I never got to ask—"

The ground vibrated with a familiar rumble and the Underworld darkened around us. Panic flooded me and I grabbed Maia by the wrist, pulling her towards the mansion. "You have to go. Now!"

"What?" She looked flustered, reluctant to move. "Did I do something wrong?"

"Get. Out!" I shoved her towards the house but it was too late.

The shadows rippled and four large paws hit the

patio, manifesting out of thin air. His claws shrieked into the metal floor, scraping up curls of golds. Cerberus roared, the hellfire within him pulsing and turning the heat up unbearable. If he didn't like me, he would have scorched us both without hesitation.

He directed himself to Maia, one massive paw raised.

"Cerberus! Down!" I called, pushing his leg to get him out of the way. "Sit!"

Some of his ears tweaked at the sound of my voice but he swiped his claws down nonetheless. I shoved Maia out of the way, taking the hit myself. A sharp pain shot up my arm as he tore my skin to shreds with his sharp nails.

The hellhound recoiled immediately when he realised he hurt me and his three heads lowered to the ground. He released a little whine and looked back up at me with his most apologetic eyes, his body shrinking as he attempted to hide under a plant.

"Penelope!" Maia hurried towards me, entirely ignoring the cowering hellhound. She touched my arm and gasped at the gashes. "Oh, this looks bad."

"It's fine," I groaned, trying not to move too much. The scratches stung and more blood welled up and trickled on the path. "I'm fine."

"You're not." She ushered me inside, her

demeanour stern and befitting of the ruler of the Underworld. She gestured to my usual chair in the sun parlour. "Sit."

I obeyed reluctantly. I wasn't used to people bossing me around but it was kind of nice to have her fussing over me. It had been a long time since anyone took care of me like this, a long time since I allowed someone.

"I'm going to get something for your arm. Do you have bandages or should I get a doctor or—" She looked around, searching for something. Her gaze landed on the cowering hellhound in the corner and she glared at him. "Come, I can't leave you alone with him."

"No, don't worry, it's okay. He didn't mean to hurt me." I shot the guilty dog a look. "He just doesn't like the Hadeses."

"Ah, I see." She pointed at the three-headed dog. "Stay."

He whimpered in return but remained still.

Interesting. He didn't usually obey anyone that wasn't me, least of all a Hades.

"Bandages?" Maia repeated, her hands firmly on her hips.

"Through the door on the left, last door in the hallway you should find the supply closet. Or I can wake Remus."

"No, don't wake anyone. I'll be right back." She gave me a stern look. "Don't. Move."

"Yes, Your Darkness," I teased, earning another, even sterner look.

I didn't know she could be this bossy and I caught myself watching her leave. The natural authority was attractive on her, not that I should notice. She was the last person I should be noticing.

Once she was gone, I turned my attention back to Cerberus. I held out my good hand, urging him close. "Come here, you silly boy."

He crawled over, his three heads whimpering as he curled against my leg. Despite shrinking, he was still a massive beast that took up most of the sun room. His large fangs descended from his mouths and his red eyes glowed in the fading light, but he was the cutest dog to me.

I patted his three heads, scratching all of his ears equally. "It's okay, I'm not mad at you. I know it was an accident."

Cer carefully licked the open wounds on my arm, lapping away the blood and soothing the sting.

"Good boy. It's okay. Just promise you'll be nicer to Maia, okay?"

The three heads growled softly.

"Cerberus," I warned him.

He whined and returned to licking my arm, each

head taking turns. They paused when Maia returned and two of them growled protectively.

Maia hesitated for a moment but walked straight past him, not paying him any attention. She pulled one of the chairs towards mine and patted the table. I put my arm up for her and she doused it with stinging disinfectant.

I hissed.

"Sorry." She rubbed some soothing cream on it, her dainty fingers gentle over the wounds. Once she was satisfied, she wrapped a bandage around my arm. And another. And another.

"That's probably enough," I said, briefly touching the top of her hand to stop her. "You've turned me into a mummy."

She chuckled. "It's appropriate, you're in the land of the dead."

"But I'm not dead and we're not Egyptian."

"Right." A pensive look filled her eyes as she stared at my arm. "I'm surprised you can get hurt in the Underworld. This will heal, won't it?"

"Yes, it will. Perks of being alive."

She adjusted her blouse. "And if it had been a fatal blow?"

"Then I'd have just ended up back here. Only dead this time so not a big deal. I suppose I'd have had to give up my position as Persephone, I'm not entirely sure. It doesn't really matter, I'm here for eternity, so." I stood up from my chair, gesturing at the empty table. "Shall I get the wine? I don't want to be a bad host."

She chuckled and pointed back at my seat. "I'll get it. You sit. Where is the wine?"

"In the cellar. Cerberus will escort you." I laughed when I saw face fell. "It's a joke. I'll show you."

"I told you to sit."

"Only my arm is hurt, I can still walk," I protested, enjoying getting a rise out of her.

She blocked my path, her lips tugged up in a knowing smile. She pressed one finger against my chest, slowly pushing me back. "Sit."

My chest tightened from the sudden proximity and Maia's eyes darkened when she noticed my hitching breath. Her gaze flicked down to my lips and hers slightly parted, an irresistible invitation. I found myself leaning in at the same time as she was inching towards me. Her warm breath tickled my lip and a little shiver tingled down my spine.

I jolted back. "We shouldn't."

Maia released a tempered breath, her cheeks flushed red. Flustered, it took a moment for her to step back. She smiled politely but the desire still lingered in her gaze. "You're right, I'm sorry, I don't know what came over me. That shouldn't have happened."

"I'm sorry too, that was incredibly unprofessional of me," I said, not wanting her to take the full blame for what almost happened. I had leaned in too.

"I should go," Maia said, already moving towards the door. She paused once she was at a safe distance. "Are you going to be okay? With your arm?"

"Yes, I'll be fine. How are you getting home? Do you want a ride in my carriage?"

She held up her hand as she fled. "No, I'll call my own. Goodnight, Penelope."

I sank back in my chair and released a long, frustrated sigh. This was not how I meant tonight to go.

The sound of a door opening pulled me out of my thoughts and for a moment, I thought Maia had returned. My hopes fell when another woman waltzed into the mansion like she owned it and I sank back into my chair. "What are you doing here?"

Molly flashed me a coquettish smile. "What do you mean? I work here."

"You don't work at the mansion, you're my assistant." I played with my bandage. "What happened to your holiday?"

"I decided to cut it short." She sat down in the chair Maia just vacated and gestured back to the front doors. "Was that Hades I just saw leaving?"

"It was."

"What was she doing here?"

"I invited her over for a drink, not that it's any of your business."

Concern flitted over Molly's face but she quickly covered it up with a shrug. "I hope you know what you're doing."

"And what is it you think I'm doing?" I bit back.

"Jeopardising your position and everything you've worked for. I haven't heard you say a good word about any of the Hadeses for as long as we've been down here. Be wise, okay?"

Her logic only annoyed me more. "Don't talk to me about being the Persephone. What I've worked for all these years is balance in the Underworld and serving the dead. If Maia and I can work toge—"

"Maia?" Molly scoffed. "So you're on a first name basis now?"

"Jealousy doesn't look good on you."

"I'm not jealous. You're not the only one who has worked hard to run this place but hey, if you don't want my advice, even though I've been your assistant for a literal century, then fine, do whatever you want. But don't come running back to me when things inevitably fall apart." She spun on her heels, her snakes hissing angrily at me.

I rose from my chair too, grabbing her by the wrist. "Wait."

She sighed dramatically and turned back around. "What? Hey, what happened to your arm?"

"You're right, I've not been doing this on my own." I said, ignoring her question. I released the other woman's arm, not wanting to give her the wrong impression. "I'm being unfair to you and I apologise."

"Thank you." Molly looked at me, her eyes softening. "Look, I'm not going to deny it. I'm a little jealous but it's not like we're great loves or anything. We just used each other to pass the time. It gets boring here without a little something."

"You were a little more to pass the time," I told her sincerely.

She smiled but the snakes in her hair didn't echo the sentiment. "Let's not let our past ruin things. We've always worked well together and I want to continue doing that, even if that means redefining what that means."

"Are you sure?"

"Yes. You know I have my own reasons for sticking around and I'm a little intrigued about the new Hades. If you see something in her, maybe there is something. I want to be around for that." She held out her hand, rattling the gold bracelets around her wrist. "Truce?"

I took her hand in mine. "Truce."

She leaned in and pressed a soft but meaningful kiss on my cheek. "Goodnight, Persephone."

A twinge of sadness passed through me as she left but it didn't linger. If anything, I was relieved that we got a chance to talk and straighten this out. I was going to need my assistant if the Underworld stood a chance of improving and for once, I felt like that was actually possible.

FOURTEEN

MAIA

I PAUSED in front of the temple, seriously considering turning around and bailing on the meeting with Penelope. I didn't want to see her, not after I made a fool of myself. Why was I always attracted to the wrong people? Of all the people I could be drawn to, why did it have to be Persephone? *The* Persephone.

"Your Darkness?" Stephan said, pausing next to me. "Everything alright?"

"Yes, I'm fine. I'm going in but you don't need to come with me."

Surprise flitted through his eyes. "Are you sure?"

"Yes." I nodded, glad he didn't ask for an explanation. I walked in by myself, mentally preparing my apology for how we left things last. Hopefully, her opinion of me hadn't fallen too much.

I arrived to an empty meeting room and with a glance at the large clock above the hearth, I sat down on my throne. I didn't have to wait long for the door on the other side to open and my traitorous heart fluttered when I saw Penelope.

The butterflies quickly died when her gorgon assistant followed her in and I sank back in my chair, disappointed that we weren't going to be alone. Maybe that was for the best though.

"Hello," Penelope said, sitting down across from me. She held out her hand for her red planner, not once looking me in the eye. "My apologies for being late."

"You're not late, I was early."

"You're kind. Let's start right away. Do you have the reports for me?"

"I do." I handed her my folder, making sure our hands didn't touch accidentally. "I also have a proposition for you."

She finally looked at me, intrigue flashing across her face. "I'm listening."

"After we talked about the Terminal, I spoke to my advisors to see if we could hire more people but we don't have the budget for that."

Penelope scoffed lightly. "Why am I not surprised?"

"I wasn't finished yet. I don't think the issue is the lack of staff. I've observed the Terminal and crunched the numbers. There are plenty of people doing nothing or doing things badly. There's no communication, the rules in the handbook only work on paper, it's just so inefficient."

"I'm aware, you don't need to tell me that." She clicked her pen impatiently. "You said you had a proposal? What is it?"

"A training program that both sides attend together, particularly for the workers at the Terminal. On top of that, I want to create a singular body of authority."

"There is a singular body of authority, it's you."

"No, I mean a joint one. One that has representatives of both sides and that your people and my people have to report to. I know it'll take time to introduce a new system but I'm not in a hurry. We have plenty of time to figure this out, right?"

Penelope stared at me, her expression unreadable. She crossed her arms tightly across her chest, her eyes never leaving me. "You're asking a lot from my side but I can see the benefits. What is in it for you though? What you're suggesting sounds like a loss of power for your side."

I knew she was going to ask me that question. "I'm not here to squabble about power. I want to do what's right for the denizens of the Underworld. I had my advisors draw up the numbers and create a plan for this project. It's all in the file, please look at it and tell me if you can see this working."

The other woman gingerly touched the folder and nodded. "I will. I want us to work together on things."

"Me too." I glanced at her hovering assistant, wishing she wasn't here so I could speak freely.

Penelope noticed and handed my report to her. "Can you get this to my advisors?"

"Right now?" the gorgon asked, the snakes in her hair lowering curiously.

"Yes, right now. I'll see you back at the Mansion," Penelope said, her tone gentle but commanding at the same time. It was clear there was no room for discussion and with a slight bow, her assistant left through the heavy door on their side.

Locked in tense silence, Penelope and I stared at each other for a moment. Not able to take the awkwardness, I rose from my seat and pretended to check out the massive clock above the hearth. It was easier to compose myself with my back towards her.

The rhythmic ticking of the clock soothed some of my nerves and finally, I turned. Penelope was exactly where I left her, seated in her throne with the authority and confidence that would give the original Persephone a run for her money.

She broke the silence first. "I've been meaning to thank you for the coffee. It was a wonderfully thoughtful gift."

"You're welcome, you said you missed it."

"I do."

"I've asked the person who fulfils my Overworld orders to stop by your Mansion before she passes on the list. Please make use of the service as much as you want."

Penelope raised one of her perfect eyebrows. "Really?"

"Yes. There's no reason why you have to be deprived of anything. That's your right as the living." I gathered a breath. "I also wanted to apologise again for my behaviour when we saw each other last."

"There's no need."

"There is. I acted rashly and impulsively and I don't want to mess this up. I know how important it is for you that the Hades takes their role seriously and I do. Therefore, nothing should happen between us. Not that I think something is going to happen, I know what I'm feeling is one-sided, but I just wanted to clear things up. I want to be the Hades you deserve."

A little smile tugged Penelope's red lips up as she gracefully rose from her chair. "And I appreciate that. I appreciate you."

"I'm glad, that's so important to me."

"Good." She joined me by the hearth, standing just a little closer than necessary. "And it's not one-sided."

A blazing heat awoke in my stomach and my knees grew weak from her intense gaze. I forcibly swallowed the lump in my throat. "It's not?"

"No, but I agree with you. Nothing should happen," she said, her voice low.

"So we're in agreement."

She nodded, stepping even closer. "Exactly."

The air crackled with anticipation and as much as I wanted to kiss her, knew it was a bad idea. My breath hitched as our lips brushed together, the charged tension awakening all the butterflies in my stomach. There was barely a hair of distance between us and yet, I couldn't bring myself to bridge the gap.

"We shouldn't," I murmured, trailing a finger up her slender arm.

She released a little sigh, her warm breath tickling my skin. "We shouldn't."

"I should go," I said, not moving a muscle. I couldn't if I wanted to. Her presence erased any rational thoughts and left me with an overwhelming desire that wouldn't let me out of its grip.

Penelope moved some of my hair over my shoulder, exposing my neck. She brushed her hand over my collarbone and up to my jaw, her touch searingly hot. "Or…"

Unable to resist, I closed the minuscule gap between us and crashed my lips on hers. Her breath hitched and her arms immediately tangled around me, pulling me flush to her. Encouraged by her enthusiasm, I parted my mouth, desperate for more. After months of dancing around each other and denying my feelings, I was losing all my composure and control.

The other woman sucked my bottom lip in and she moaned when our tongues met. Her hand found the zipper on the back of my dress and I jolted back, breaking the kiss. "We shouldn't."

She sucked in a breath, not able to hide the disappointment flashing through her eyes. "You're probably right."

"Not here, anyway," I blurted, completely undermining everything I just said.

Amusement flickered through her darkened eyes. I was standing so close, I could see the silver flecks in them. She leaned in for a slower more intimate kiss, her mouth warm and supple. "Where then?"

Looking at the beautiful woman in my arms, I knew it was futile to try and resist. I wanted her, more than I wanted anything else in the moment. I could deny myself but it wouldn't stop whatever this was, only prolong the chase. Eventually, we'd end up in this exact position, I was sure of it.

"Somewhere more appropriate," I said, suddenly acutely aware of our surroundings.

She released a crystal laugh. "I believe this is where the original Hades and Persephone had their honeymoon. Where else would be more appropriate?"

"Right. We're Hades and Persephone." The reality of the situation washed over me and I took a reluctant step back. "This is never going to be uncomplicated, is it?"

"It can be, if we make it so."

"But it won't be." I adjusted my dress and flattened my hair so it didn't look like someone just ran their hands through it. "Not if we jump in impulsively and mess things up."

Penelope gathered a breath, the haze slowly disappearing from her eyes. "You're right. Why don't you come over for dinner so we can talk about this? We'll sit at a normal-sized table, have that nice red wine I promised you, and we'll talk."

I nodded, relief softening the tight knots in my stomach. "I'd like that."

She briefly touched my hip before stepping back, breaking the spell she had over me. "It's a date."

FIFTEEN

Maia

THE CARRIAGE CAME to a shaky halt in front the Golden Mansion and for once, the rising nausea in my stomach wasn't due to the tumultuous ride. The driver held his thumbs up questioningly and I returned the gesture. Even if it was still too fast for my liking, it was a lot better than it used to be. Maybe in a few years, it would be an acceptable speed.

Nerves jittered through me as I approached the ostentatious building. I couldn't decide if this was worse than my castle or not. Neither felt like a place to live in.

The golden front doors swung open before I could knock and a man in a stiff suit welcomed me in. "This way, Your Darkness. Her Greatness is waiting for you in the dining room."

"Thank you." I followed him into the mansion, trying not to pay attention to the reflective walls. I was already worried enough about how I looked, I didn't need to see it a hundred times around me.

He opened a set of double doors and my breath hitched at the sight of Penelope waiting in the middle of the room. She turned, her grey dress accentuating her natural curves. "Evening."

"Hi."

She smiled at the servant. "Thank you, Remus. You can retire for the evening."

He bowed slightly and I could tell how much respect he held for her just in the way he carried himself around her. It only made me admire her more. Remus closed the doors on his way out, leaving the two of us in the dining room.

"Would you like a drink before dinner?" Penelope proposed, gesturing to the little cart with all kinds of bottles of liquor.

I nodded in my approach. "Yes, please."

"Anything in particular?" she asked, picking up an empty glass.

"Surprise me."

"Adventurous."

"I told you I like trying new things," I returned, hoping I was coming across half as interesting as she was.

"So do I, although there's also comfort in routine and monotony." She prepared two amber drinks with ice and handed me one, our fingers brushing against each other. "To our health, considering we're still alive."

"To our health," I toasted, gently clinking my glass against hers. I took a sip from the floral drink, surprised by the perfect balance of sweet and bitter. "This is delicious although I don't recognise the flavour."

"The Underworld has a lot to offer." She gestured to the little salon in the corner. "Shall we sit?"

I nodded in agreement and occupied one of the velvet chaises, disappointed by how far we were sitting apart. To hide my discomfort, I took another sip from my drink and put it on the glass table between us. "I never got to ask why you're down here."

"It's a boring story," she said.

"I doubt it." I crossed my legs, trying to get more comfortable in the chair. "Please, I'm curious."

"Well, I was brought up in one of Demeter's and

the priestesses prepared us all for diverse positions. I ended up getting a taste for this one."

"Interesting. I heard it's really hard to get into Demeter's temple. They must've realised you were going to be special."

"No, nothing like that. One of the high priestesses found me when I was a baby. She always claimed I was born from the tears of a white calf but I think that was just a story to cheer me up so I didn't feel bad about not having parents." She smiled at me over the rim of her glass.

"That's quite a story. Uncommon but not unheard of it though," I smiled. "It could be true."

"It seems unlikely. Anyway, even though I grew up in the temple, I never felt like I fit in."

"So naturally, you took a job in the Underworld," I teased.

"I don't know why you're laughing, you're here too." She set her empty glass on the table. "Do you ever regret it?"

"No, I don't. I worry about it, but I don't regret it," I admitted.

"Worry? What do you worry about?"

"A variety of things. Not being good enough, not doing things right, disappointing the dead." I hesitated. "Disappointing you."

"Me?" Surprise raised her voice.

"Hmm-hmm. I admire you and the way you run this place. My first priority is making sure I live up to my title and doing right by our guests," I explained, finishing my drink too and setting the glass next to hers. "I won't lie, I took this job on a whim but I want to do it justice."

"I can tell. I admire you too. You've already done more for the Underworld in the short time you were here than all the Hadeses of the past century." She rose from her seat and gestured to the table. "I hope you're hungry."

"I am." I followed her, taking to the seat opposite of her. Just like dinner at my place, the food was waiting for us under golden domes but it was a reasonable amount of platters and we could actually see each other.

We filled our plates in amicable silence, passing serving spoons between us.

"Everything looks delicious," I said, taking my first bite from a confusing green vegetable.

"I have good cooks." Penelope gestured to a little gravy boat with red sauce. "You should try the specialty of the house. Pomegranate sauce."

I chuckled. "Really?"

"Hmm. It's the original Persephone's recipe."

"Then I have to try it," I said, picking up the jug and pouring some on my plate and releasing a fruity aroma. I dipped some of my meat into the red sauce and ate it, surprised by the depth of flavour. "Wow. That's delicious. I'd have stayed in the Underworld for that."

"I know, right?" The other woman snapped her fingers. "Wine. I'm not letting you leave without trying it this time."

I contemplated making a cheeky remark but I was barely holding my nerves together, I wasn't sure if I was ready for *the* conversation of the evening.

Penelope poured us two glasses of wine and I took my first sip, not particularly impressed by the taste. It tasted slightly tangy with a hint of sweetness. Nothing special and I couldn't help but wonder if the wine had always been a ruse.

"Where's Cerberus?" I inquired between bites.

"He's being watched," she assured me. "I'm sorry that he attacked you last time."

"Hey, you're the one that got hurt. Can I ask you something though?"

She finished her food and folded her cutlery on her plate. "Go ahead."

"Why is he not guarding the gates of the Underworld?" I ate my last piece of meat and wiped my mouth on the napkin. "I asked around and it appears he hasn't for many centuries."

"That's a good question." Penelope rose from her

seat. "Shall we get more comfortable? I had the sunroom set up for us so we could have some of your wonderful coffee, although there's admittedly little sun."

We retreated to the parlour where true to her word, there was hot coffee waiting next to two comfortable ear chairs facing each other. I sat down in one while Penelope sat down in the other, a little smile playing around her lips. She'd orchestrated the entire evening and I could tell she was enjoying it running as planned.

I picked up the hot mug she prepared for me and eagerly sipped the bitter drink. "So, Cerberus?" I asked.

"Right. Well, as you can tell, he can be a little… wild and unruly. One of the past Hadeses, way before my term, seemed discontent with managing the hellhound and locked him up to get him out of the way." She pensively drank from her steaming cup and sighed. "I found him and decided to take him in. It's been quite a challenging venture but I couldn't stand having him locked up."

I nodded, considering everything she just told me. "Do you think he'd be willing to return to his post?"

Surprise flitted over her face. "I'm not sure. He's grown a real distaste for the Hades, but you experienced that first hand. But I'm sure he could learn to trust again, if someone was willing to put in the effort."

"I am," I assured her. "I just want the Underworld to run like it's meant to and have everyone in their rightful place."

She chuckled slightly. "You're preaching to the choir."

"I know. I think we can make that happen, together," I said. I wasn't sure where I got my confidence from but something about Penelope made me believe we could do it.

Penelope set her mug down. "I think so too. If you're committed to helping Cerberus, I'll help you with that. Make sure he doesn't tear you to shreds."

"I appreciate that." My laughter gradually ebbed away and left me with a warm glow in my chest. Recognising the feeling, I rose from the seat so I could look at the view of her beautiful gardens instead of at her. "I really appreciate all the help and your patience while I find my feet. I know it can't be easy to have so many Hadeses pass through."

"I usually don't bother, it's a lot of wasted energy," Penelope said, joining me by the window. She placed a gentle hand on my arm, urging me to look at her. Her dark eyes shimmered. "Most of the time."

My chest fluttered. "But not this time?"

"No, I don't believe so." She leaned in and pressed a wonderfully tender kiss on my lips. She tasted of coffee and pomegranates, a strange combination that suited her.

Butterflies awoke in my stomach and I felt lighter than air as they fluttered through me. I eagerly kissed her back, not able to remember why I thought this was a bad idea in the first place. Everything between us felt so natural even if it was new. It just felt right.

A clattering sound drew my attention and I gasped. "It's raining. I didn't realise it rained down here!"

Penelope's bemused face lit up the room. "Of course, it does."

I threw the sliding door open and grabbed her hand, pulling her out into the night. "Come on!"

"What are you doing?" she called, resisting only for good measure.

Thick drops of rain fell on my face, tickling my skin. "It's hot!"

Penelope laughed as she pulled me into her, her hands falling on my hips. Water streamed down her face, wetting her hair and staining her grey dress dark. "You're ridiculous," she mused affectionately.

"How can you have so much fun in the land of the dead?"

"Because I'm not dead," I shouted back. "I'm alive. You're alive!"

Her gaze smouldered as it settled on me. She pulled me in, capturing me in a determined kiss that set me ablaze. The warmth of the rain melted with the searing heat of her mouth and I drowned in her, the desire in my belly growing with every caress and every breath. Butterflies grew rampant in my chest and I barely remembered to breathe. I just wanted her like I hadn't wanted anyone before.

She pulled away, leaving the space of a breath between us. "I want to do this with you, Maia."

"This?" I asked, barely able to hear her under the heavy pour.

Penelope tugged me along to one of the open sheds. The falling rain played percussion on the roof but it wasn't nearly as deafening as standing in the middle of it.

She brushed her thumb along my bottom lip. "I smudged your lipstick. And got some of mine on you too."

"I would think so with the intensity of how you kissed me," I blurted, feeling uncharacteristically daring.

She chuckled, her eyes flickering with intense

emotion. "You're so vibrant, Maia. So full of life. When I'm with you, I can feel it."

"Feel what?"

"The sun." She kissed me again, soft and tender this time. "I want to do this with you."

"This?"

Penelope's voice caught with excitement. "Whatever this is. Ruling together, us together. I want to take a chance. It's so not like me but there's just something about you. I can't resist it. I don't want to. You're a breath of fresh air and I want to see where this will take us."

Her declaration released the flood of emotions I was holding back and I allowed them to flow through me. I pulled her into a kiss, determined to show her how much I wanted this too. Maybe people would find it unconventional that we were getting together but down in the Underworld, nothing felt more normal to me. We were the Hades and Persephone after all.

SIXTEEN

MAIA

"Morning," Penelope trailed a light finger along my spine, her touch warm and ticklish.

I turned to look at her, not bothering to cover up. Instead, my attention was taken up by the beautiful woman right next to me, a wonderful first thing to see in the morning. "You're awake."

"Hmm-hmm." She leaned on her elbow, her hair messy and wild. "How did you sleep?"

"Barely," I chuckled, unsure whether it was appropriate to kiss her or not. I felt like we decided something last night but there was a difference between agreeing to start a relationship and kissing in the morning.

I sat up against the headboard, taking in the room. It was elegant but impersonal without little touches or trinkets to reflect the owner of the Mansion. Empty.

"What time is it?" I asked, twisting out of the bed so I could reach my crumpled dress on the floor.

"Early."

The sheets behind me rustled and I felt Penelope's warmth before I her hands trailed up my back. She pressed a kiss on my shoulder and I relaxed into her touch, allowing myself to indulge for one more moment before it was back to reality. I turned and captured her in a lazy kiss, savouring the tenderness. The movement of her lips brought back memories of the night and all the places on my body she kissed, teased, and pleased.

"I should go," I told her, reluctantly pulling away. "Which way would you like me to leave? I imagine you probably don't want your entire household to find out I spend the night."

Penelope watched me, her eyes following me as I gathered my things through the room. "I don't mind. You can have breakfast here or I can sneak you out. Whichever you're most comfortable with."

"Really? You want to have breakfast with me?"

She shrugged, letting the covers fall away. "Why not?"

I slipped my dress back on and turned, hoping she would do my zipper up. "And you wouldn't care if you servants saw me?"

"No, this is my home." She pressed her warm body into me, her arms wrapping around me. Her lips tickled the shell of my ear, her breath hot. "Inside these walls, I get to be me and do what I want."

"And outside?" I asked, turning to examine her.

"Out there I play the part of Persephone. It's still me but a curated version of me."

"Ah." I stepped back, trying to unravel my ball of feelings. "Yeah, I understand. I like to keep certain things *curated* too. I should go." I grabbed my heels and wrestled them on, almost falling over. I wasn't sure why I was frustrated, it wasn't like she said anything unreasonable and yet, I was feeling the urge to storm out.

"Maia, Maia, Maia." Penelope chased after me, grabbing me before I could leave her chambers. "Stop."

"What?" I snapped, a little harsher than I intended.

"I'm not saying I want to keep this a secret. I just don't want to do anything we're not comfortable with. I don't know about you, but I've never been a making-out-in-public-person."

"Me either."

She drew me in for a kiss, holding me close. "But I also don't want to hide. What other people say about me is none of my business. Okay?"

"Okay." I relaxed in her arms, not sure why this was affecting me like this. I didn't want to broadcast this either, it was too new, too fresh, and there was too much at stake. Still, I appreciated us being able to talk about this. "I don't think I'm quite ready for breakfast but I'll leave through the front door."

Penelope nodded, kissing me again before she opened the door. "I'll walk you out."

I worried about someone giving us a weird look on our way back to the front door but nobody even batted an eye. Maybe it wasn't all that weird to have the Hades and Persephone under the same roof or maybe they knew to mind their own business.

"I had a lovely night," I said, smoothing out my hair in one of my many reflections.

"Me too." She pecked my lips. "I'll see you soon."

It wasn't a question and I liked her confidence on the matter. "I'll see you soon," I confirmed, stepping out of the mansion. I wasn't sure why I expected bright sunlight, maybe it just felt right after being inside for so long, but the morning was only a shade lighter than the previous evening.

I took my carriage back to the castle, barely noticing the shaking and wobbling. I was too lost in thoughts of the memories of the night and the curiosity of how things were going to play out.

Stephan greeted me at the entrance, his suit crisp and his expression neutral. "Welcome back, Your Darkness. Breakfast in the Grey Hall?"

My stomach grumbled and I nodded, pleased there wasn't an interrogation or search party waiting on this end. "Yes, thank you. Anything happen while I was gone?"

"No, everything is exactly as it should be." He opened the doors of the Grey Hall for me. "Enjoy your morning, Your Darkness."

I filled my plate with my favourite things while humming a little song to myself. Everything tasted just a little sweeter this morning but I was pretty sure that had nothing to do with the food.

Once I was finished, I retreated to my study to prepare my upcoming meetings and go over the rest of my reports. Even though Penelope and I were clearly getting on, that wasn't going to be enough to get the Underworld running again. It needed solid investment and time on my account with some drastic changes that had to be made very carefully.

Towards the evening, a knock sounded on the closed doors and Erebus entered with a bow. "I apologise for disturbing you but Persephone is requesting to see you."

I looked up from my file. "Sorry? Penelope is here? Why?"

"She didn't say, Your Darkness."

"Let her in. I'll receive her in my office," I said, quickly checking my reflection in the paperknife. I rose from my desk so I could meet her by the door only to change my mind and sit down in the little salon. That felt too casual so I jumped back up to return to my desk where I'd look all powerful.

The doors opened again and Penelope strode in, exuding confidence in every step. Now that was power.

"Your Darkness," she teased, her eyes flickering with amusement.

"Your Greatness," I returned, waiting for Erebus to leave before I rose up. "What brings you here?"

She placed a file on my desk, her smirk never wavering. "I realised I forgot to hand you this file during our last meeting."

"Ah, so this is work related?" I grinned, joy sparking in my chest. Even I could see through a thin ruse like that. I joined Penelope on the other side of my desk, leaving a respectable gap between us. "Couldn't find a single messenger in that Mansion of yours?"

"No, this document is far too important, I had to deliver it personally. Building a good working relationship with you is a priority to me," she remarked, reaching out to me. She trailed her fingers up my arm, her touch light but surprisingly intimate. "Unless you prefer a courier next time?"

Feeling brave, I closed the gap and kissed her mouth, lingering for only a fraction of the time I wanted to. "No, if it's important it's better if you come yourself."

"I'm glad you see it that way because we'll be seeing a lot of each other."

I smiled against her lips, a warm glow settling over me. I'd never expected to fall in love in the Underworld but I welcomed it with open arms. I wanted to make this work and we had eternity to figure it out. Together.

SEVENTEEN

Maia

WAKING up next to a sleeping Penelope was quickly becoming a familiar sight. The beautiful woman stirred next to me, pulling the duvet to her side so I had nothing left. With a sigh, I grabbed the spare blanket from the bottom of the bed. After a few months, I'd gotten used to her hogging the covers.

Sleep eluded me and I slipped out of bed, tiptoeing to the large window of my bed chambers. I pulled the dark curtains back, inviting the faint light into the room. The green mist hanging over the Underworld was a familiar sight by now and it didn't bother me, but I knew Penelope suffered from the lack of sunlight.

While I admired the view, the sheets behind me rustled and footsteps sounded on the cold floor. Two warm arms snaked around my waist and tightened around me. "Morning," Penelope breathed, her chin resting on my shoulder.

"Hi," I murmured, the butterflies rising now she was awake. I snuggled into her embrace, her touch familiar and comforting. "Did I wake you?"

"Yes, but it's fine. I need to get back to the Mansion." She sighed at the view. "Wow, it looks like it's miserable weather again."

"It always is." I turned in her arms and pressed a soft kiss on her lips. "Are you sure you don't want to have breakfast together?"

Penelope yawned and scratched the side of her face. "No, I've already slept over twice, I need to get back. I can't get too distracted by this and forget to do my job."

"This?" I repeated teasingly.

The usually confident woman averted her gaze, her cheeks flushing. "Our relationship."

"You're adorable." I pressed another kiss on her lips and untangled myself from her, albeit reluctantly. She was right, we had a busy day ahead and while this was a great start, we couldn't get lost in each other. Even if we wanted to.

"We should get dressed," she said, reaching for her clothes from last night. Her blue dress rippled like water, the supple fabric cascading down her body. Even if I wanted to, I couldn't look away from the beautiful woman. Contentment glowed warm in my chest as I watched her get ready for the day.

"I can feel you looking at me," Penelope quipped despite having her back turned to me.

I chuckled, resting on the bed. "Am I not allowed to look?"

She turned around and pressed a kiss on my lips. "You're allowed. But you should get dressed too."

"I was distracted watching you," I admitted.

She laughed and gave me a gentle push towards my wardrobe. "Go on. Hurry. We have an Underworld to run. Don't be late to our meeting."

"I wouldn't dare."

She left me with a kiss that lingered through breakfast and the first meeting with my advisors. Things had certainly settled around me and everything was a lot easier now I had Penelope's support and encouragement. The open communication and her expertise were invaluable and it surprised everyone how quickly things turned around. It was almost like the first Hades and Persephone knew what they were doing when they decided to rule the Underworld together. It was a shame it had taken this long to reinstate their original methods although I couldn't imagine we were the first to follow in their footsteps and fall in love.

Once my advisors were gone, Stephan arrived with a polite bow. "Your carriage awaits."

"Thank you, I'm ready to go." I followed him outside where the black horses were waiting for me, impatient as always. I climbed in the chariot, shuffling to the side so there was enough space for him. "Any news from Olympus?" I asked as we set in motion.

He shook his head. "Not yet but I'm expecting the answer any moment."

"Zeus better not deny my request. I really want to make this happen," I grumbled, holding my stomach to fight the growing nausea. One day, I'd get used to this.

The carriage pulled up to the temple and I entered eagerly, looking forward to seeing Penelope again even though we hadn't been apart for very long.

The other woman was already waiting in her throne, with her assistant standing behind her.

Penelope crossed her arms and challengingly raised an eyebrow. "You're late."

"No, you're early." I sat down in my seat, no longer intimidated by her act. If anything, I found it hot.

We exchanged folders.

"Reports from my side. The processing numbers at the Terminal are up. It's not by much yet, but it's something. Thank you for lending me extra manpower from your side, it's making a real difference," I said, accepting hers. "You?"

"Numbers are down on my side but that was to be expected," she replied, flicking through my file. "Complaints are up as well but nothing to be concerned about. People always fight against new systems, even if it'll benefit them."

"Yes, same. I'm sure it'll settle once they realise it's better and after we hire more people that never knew the old system." I looked at the beautiful woman opposite of me, finding it hard not to admire her openly. "How's Cerberus getting on?"

"Good. We had a little mishap yesterday with a trainer but nobody got hurt. I'm sure he'll get the hang of it soon, he's just a little out of practice."

I nodded understandingly. "It'll be good if I no longer need to employ guards so we can allocate the budget to another branch but no rush. I've also spoken to Styx and he agreed to double his cleaning efforts. That should help with the pollution of the river."

"Excellent."

A knock came from the door on my side and surprise flitted through me. My people knew better than to disturb me during one of these meetings.

"Come in," I called, glancing at Penelope if she knew what this was about but she looked just as confused.

Stephan entered, his face shimmering with excitement. He bowed deeply towards Penelope before handing me a thick envelope with a lightning bolt on the seal. "Zeus' reply. I assumed you wouldn't want to wait."

"I don't," I said, immediately tearing through the seal. Elation grew in my chest when I found the invitation I'd hoped for. "Yes!"

"What is it?" Penelope inquired as politely as she could. I knew she was dying of curiosity inside.

"Something wonderful," I grinned, turning to Stephan. "Thank you."

He left with a bow and catching on, Penelope dismissed Molly too. The gorgon obeyed with a lot less glaring my way than she did originally. Not that I blamed her.

Once she was gone, Penelope joined me by the hearth and pressed a kiss on my shoulder. "Hi."

"Hey." I turned to kiss her properly, savouring the moment alone. While the nights were ours, it was rare to have time alone during the day with her. "What happened to not getting distracted by *this*."

"You're so annoying when you echo my words back to me," she said, her grin betraying how she really felt about it. "Are you going to tell me what this letter is? Why is Zeus writing to you?"

"I actually wrote to him." I held out the envelope. "Here, that should explain everything."

She quietly read the card. "It's an invite to the yearly party at Peak Olympus. What's so special about that? The Hades goes to that every year. Oh, I suppose this is your first one."

I chuckled, gesturing to the envelope. "There's another invite."

Penelope pulled the second card out and dropped it like it burned her. She brought a trembling hand to her mouth, muffling a strangled sob. "W-What is this? Maia? What did you do?"

Worry tightened my chest as I picked up the envelope, unsure what to do with the invitation addressed to her. "I'm sorry, I should've told you about it sooner but I didn't want to get your hopes up. I thought you'd be happy. Shit. Sorry, I didn't mean to make you cry."

She swatted my arm before pulling me into the tightest hug. "You idiot. This is the most thoughtful thing anyone has done for me, ever."

I breathed a sigh of relief as I wrapped my arms around her. "Oh, good. I thought I did something wrong."

"No, this is wonderful. You're wonderful." She cried into me, her tears hot on my shoulder. "Is this real? Am I going up?"

I pressed a kiss on her temple and stroked her back as she sobbed in my arms. "Yes, you're going up. It's just for the party but I thought it was high time that you saw the sun again."

EIGHTEEN

Penelope

Nerves jittered through me as I climbed into the horse-drawn carriage, barely able to keep calm. I couldn't remember the last time I'd been this anxious or so excited.

"Ready?" Maia asked from inside, holding her hand out to me.

"No," I admitted, sitting down next to her. "And yes."

"Good. Better hold on to something," she said as her assistant closed the door behind me. "I've instructed my driver many times to go slow but I don't think he understands the meaning."

I released a nervous chuckle. "I think I'll manage."

"I'm sure you will," she said, taking my hand in hers. She leaned in, pressing a familiar kiss on my lips. "You look beautiful, by the way."

"You too. I like the crown," I said, gesturing to the circlet.

Maia touched her hair, her grip on me tightening as the carriage set in motion. "You don't think it looks ridiculous on me? It's part of the traditional set."

"No, I think it makes you look powerful." I pulled her closer, kissing her slowly and deliberately. "Thank you for this."

"It's only right. You shouldn't be chained to the Underworld," she said with conviction. "I'm sorry I haven't been able to restore the original deal Hades and Persephone had but I'm working on it."

A rush of affection came over me and I squeezed her hand. "Did Demeter write back to you?"

She groaned. "Yes, but he has a real stick up his, well, you know. Do you think that's a character requisite for the role?"

I laughed. "I don't think so. I met the previous Demeter when I was younger and she was lovely so it just depends from person to person."

A shock vibrated through the carriage and jolted

me from side to side, breaking us apart. We came to a halt and Maia peaked out of the curtain and smiled. "We're here."

My nerves returned in full. "We are?"

"Hmm-hmm." She offered her hand again. "Ready?"

I shook my head but took her hand anyway. This was a once-in-a-lifetime opportunity and I wasn't going to waste it.

Carefully, Maia escorted me down the set of stairs and I almost fell out, not paying any attention to the ground. My gaze was glued to the sky and the shimmering tapestry of stars. A waft of fresh air brushed through my hair and dress and filled my nose with the warm smell of summer. I inhaled deeply, wishing I could keep the smell trapped in my nose forever. How I missed it.

"You okay?" Maia asked, her hand gingerly touching the small of my back.

I nodded, not able to stop looking up at the night's sky. "It looks exactly the same as I remember."

"Some things don't change. Some things shouldn't change," she said.

I finally managed to tear my gaze back down and looked at the woman in front of me, overwhelmed with emotion. "I love you, Maia. That's never going to change."

"I love you too." She pressed the back of my hand against her lips and gestured to the large temple up ahead. "Shall we go mingle?"

With a nod, we followed the winding path up to the peak of Mount Olympus. Joyous music and laughter came from inside and the other people arriving around us. A handful bowed to Maia in acknowledgment but nobody paid any special attention to me. It was refreshing after being recognised anywhere in the Underworld.

We entered the temple and I took in the sea of people. After a hundred years, there wasn't a single person I knew and yet, it was easy enough to recognise who was who. A trio in blue robes stood near the fountain, no doubt the current ruling council of Poseidon. I always envied them for having someone to share their responsibilities with but not tonight. Not anymore.

"Hades!" someone called jovially. A man with thick eyebrows appeared in front of us, an empty glass in hand. "So glad you could make it."

Next to me, Maia visibly stiffened. "Hera."

"How wonderful to see you here. This must be your first annual Olympus ball. If you're looking for a familiar face, don't hesitate to join us over there. We always love to hear about our success stories."

Anger rose in me and I felt the burning need to defend Maia, but I kept myself in check. I held a lot of power in the Underworld but that didn't translate to the Overworld. I wasn't even part of the Olympian council.

Maia nodded curtly. "Hmm, maybe. I'm just saying hello to everyone."

Oblivious, the man slapped her on the back as he left. "Well, our door is always open. Once a Hera supporter, always a Hera supporter."

I took Maia's hand as soon as he was gone. "You alright?"

She released a shaky breath. "Yes, it's not the first time I've run into him. It's hard, it's not like he personally hurt me but I still blame him."

"And for good reason. It happened in his temple, under his nose. He should manage his people better, that's our job as deity." I glared at Hera's back, wishing I could give him a stern talking to. Before I could do something I'd regret, I picked two glasses of wine from a passing server and handed one to Maia. "Here, have a drink."

She took a shaky sip. "Mmm, this is good. I think a new Dionysus just started their term so this must be the first batch they've made."

I tasted the wine too and hummed appreciatively. "Not bad. Promising. Very close to how I remember the taste. Not exact but that's to be expected if they're new."

We moved through the room, greeting more people I didn't know here and there. Nobody seemed to realise who I was and I enjoyed being the mysterious woman on Maia's arm. It gave me the chance to take everything in at my own pace and enjoy my first time in the Overworld after more than a century.

A stunning woman in a sleek white dress waved as noticed us and I recognised her immediately. I'd seen her often enough on Molly's favourite dating show. The one and only Aphrodite.

She came our way, a knowing smile playing around her lips. "Hello, Hades. Persephone."

Surprised to be addressed and recognised, I looked at her questioningly.

Triumph flickered through Aphrodite's eyes. "Did you not think I would recognise you? Who else but the Persephone would be deserving to be on Hades' arm?"

A little taken aback, I released a sharp breath. "We're not together because of our positions."

"I know, I'm teasing. I heard through the grapevine that you were making an appearance so I looked you up so I'd be able to greet you properly. It's quite exciting to have you back in the Overworld. Penelope, is it?" she extended her hand. "Anastasia. Current Aphrodite."

"Nice to meet you," I said, reluctantly shaking. Our short interaction confused me and I didn't like people who confused me. Then again, Maia had been an enigma when we first met and that worked out pretty well.

Anastasia smiled warmly. "I didn't mean to offend, Penelope. Truly. I think it's fantastic to have the two rulers of the Underworld working together."

I decided to give her the benefit of the doubt and returned the smile. "Thank you. Maia is the best thing they could've sent down."

Next to me, Maia blushed and she gently swatted my arm. "You flatter me. You're the one that kept the Underworld running for a century without anyone's help."

"I had plenty of help. Maybe not from the Hades, but lots of people helped me," I teased, not able to tear my gaze away from her.

"You two are so adorable together." A slight sadness tainted Aphrodite's voice. "How wonderful to see true love. If only it was possible for everyone but not even the Goddess of Love can make that happen."

"But a lot of people on your dating show find a great match," Maia complimented her. "We watch it all the time."

Heat crept up to my ears. I never liked admitting I watched the Golden Apple but then again, this was Aphrodite. She'd be the last person to mock me for loving this kind of show.

Anastasia perked up, but only slightly. "Thank you, I try my best but some people just have no luck in love. Myself included. Isn't that ironic? Sorry. Listen to me blabber on about my sad love life. I should probably stop drinking before I start crying somewhere."

She flitted away and sympathy filled me. It had to be hard to be the Goddess of Love and watch people find matches without having someone themselves.

Maia squeezed my hand. "I'm so glad I found you."

"Me too," I told her earnestly, leaning in for a quick kiss.

"How are you enjoying the party so far?"

"I like it but it's a little busy. I'm not used to seeing this many deities in one place and making so much small talk. It's exhausting."

She released a sigh of relief. "I'm so glad you said that." She grabbed a bottle of wine from a passing server's tray and took me by the hand. "Come on, let's get out of here."

"Where are we going?" I asked, not caring and following her automatically.

Maia's eyes twinkled. "Does it matter?"

Laughing, we left Zeus' bustling temple and wandered along Mount Olympus with an encouraging breeze in my back. We paused on a spot overlooking the landscape underneath us and I took in the familiar sight of the Overworld and all its features. It looked so different from when I saw it last and yet, it was the same. The hills and the valleys, the winding rivers, and the surrounding oceans. Even if the houses and people were different, it was still the same Greece.

"Shall we sit?" Maia proposed, gesturing to a soft patch of grass.

I nodded, not caring about dirtying my dress. I'd gladly bring a memory of this night with me back to the Underworld.

Maia wrapped her arm around me and we sat in content silence, soaking in the brilliant night. There was so much I wanted to tell her and yet, nothing needed to be said at all. I rested my head on her shoulder, basking in her warmth as we waited together.

Chirping birds announced the rising morning and the first rays of sun climbed over the horizon, hesitantly but unstoppable all the same.

"Are you okay?" Maia asked, her concern shining through in her voice.

"Never been better," I sniffled. I touched her face and captured her in a tender kiss as the rising sun blessed me with its gentle glow. It was finally dawn.

Thank you for reading Trouble In Hades! I hope you liked Maia and Penelope's story and seeing my take on Hades and Persephone. If you enjoyed my twist on Greek mythology and are intrigued by Aphrodite's bad luck in love, join me in the next story: Apple From Aphrodite where Anastasia goes on her own dating show to find love.
Pre-order it here on your favourite retailer: https://books2read.com/applefromaphrodite

Download an extra epilogue about Maia and Penelope for free here: https://books.arizonatape.com/w0rm9ejslf

ALSO BY ARIZONA TAPE

Here are some recommendations on some of my other books you might like. My books are available on all retailers and can be requested in most public libraries.

You can find out more about each of my series on my website.

Crescent Lake Shifters

Take a leap of faith with these dragon shifters looking for love. Only a jump in the Crescent Lake will reveal the bonds of fate. A paranormal romance series. Each book follows a different couple.

The Griffin Sanctuary

Help Charlotte take care of endangered mythical animals in the Griffin Sanctuary in this urban fantasy series. Perfect for animal and mythology lovers.

Queens Of Olympus

A modern paranormal romance take on the Greek gods and their dating life; it's not *all* drama. Each book follows a different couple.

The Forked Tail

Get hungry with this urban fantasy series following demon chef Lana and gluttony demon Demi who cook and eat sin for breakfast, lunch, and dinner.

Crescent Lake Bears

Jump in the lake of love with these bear shifters looking for their fated mates. Only the crescent moon will reveal what's meant to be. A paranormal romance series. Each book follows a different couple.

Amethyst's Wand Shop Mysteries

An urban fantasy murder mystery series following a witch who teams up with a detective to solve murders. Each book includes a different murder.

Aliens And Animals

Get accidentally abducted in this Sci-Fi romance series and enjoy the miscommunication, cute animals, and charming aliens. Each book includes a different couple.

Purple Oasis

Find love and hope after the apocalypse at a sanctuary for witches, shifters, and more in this paranormal romance series. Each book follows a different couple.

For a full comprehensive list of all my books: www.

arizonatape.com/all-series

Signed Paperback & Merchandise:

You can find signed paperbacks, hardcovers, and merchandise based on my series (including stickers, magnets, badges, and more!) via my website: www.arizonatape.com/shop

My website also has a selection of free stories and books that'll give you a taste of my other works: www.arizonatape.com/free

ABOUT ARIZONA TAPE

Arizona Tape lives her dream life hanging out with her dog and writing stories all day.

Her favourite books to write are urban fantasy and paranormal romances with queer leads, stories that she wished were around when she was younger.

When she's not writing, she can be found cooking up a storm in the kitchen, watching shows that make her cry, or trying her hand at her new hobby of the week.

She currently lives in the United Kingdom with her girlfriend and her adorable dog who is the star of her newsletter.

Sign up here for adorable pictures, free books, and news about her books: www.arizonatape.com/subscribe

Follow Arizona Tape

- Website: www.arizonatape.com
- Mailing List: www.arizonatape.com/subscribe
- Facebook Page: http://facebook.com/arizonatapeauthor
- Reader Group: http://facebook.com/groups/arizonatape
- Bookbub: http://www.bookbub.com/authors/arizona-tape
- Twitter: http://twitter.com/arizonatape
- Instagram: http://instagram.com/arizonatape
- TikTok: http://www.tiktok.com/@arizonatape

Printed in Great Britain
by Amazon